Falkirk
Community
Trust

HOME LIBRARY SERVICE
TEL: 01324 506800

- 8 AUG 2016

- 9 SEP 2016
1 3 APR 2017
1 8 APR 2017
2 7 DEC 2017

Bo'ness
01506 778520

Bonnybridge
01324 503295

Denny
01324 504242

Falkirk
01324 503605

Grangemouth
01324 504690

Larbert
01324 503590

Meadowbank
01324 503870

Mobile
01324 506800

Slamannan
01324 851373

This book is due
for return on or
before the last date
indicated on the
label. Renewals
may be obtained
on application.

Falkirk Community Trust is a charity registered in Scotland, No: SC042403

FALKIRK COMMUNITY
TRUST LIBRARIES

OPERATION STORMWIND

'Operation Desert Storm' was the code-name for the Western Allies' attack on Saddam Hussein. Six years later, the Iraqi dictator plans his revenge...

Britain is planning to open a new oil field in the North Sea, serviced by the new rig 'Margaret Thatcher'. But Saddam has hired an international terrorist known as 'The Palestinian' to destroy the rig before it can become operational.

It is up to Lt. Sealham of the Special Boat Service to trace the terrorist and stop him reaching his target in the North Sea.

Please note: *This book may contain some material which may not suit all our readers.*

OPERATION STORMWIND

OPERATION STORMWIND

by

Duncan Harding

Magna Large Print Books
Long Preston, North Yorkshire,
BD23 4ND, England.

British Library Cataloguing in Publication Data.

Harding, Duncan
    Operation Stormwind.

    A catalogue record of this book is
    available from the British Library

    ISBN   0-7505-1579-1

First published in Great Britain by
Severn House Publishers Ltd., 1996

Published in Large Print 2000 by arrangement with
Severn House Publishers Ltd.

Magna Large Print is an imprint of Library Magna Books Ltd.

Printed and bound in Great Britain by
T.J. (International) Ltd., Cornwall, PL28 8RW

'Never fear! By Allah, they will regret this "Operation Desert Storm" of theirs. I shall pay them back tenfold.'

Saddam Hussein, Baghdad, 1990

PREFACE

A CALL TO ARMS

'He, the trained spy, had walked into the
 trap
For a bogus guide, seduced with the old
 tricks.'

W H Auden

The whistle shrilled. Immediately the lean hooded figure burst out of the house. He started to run full pelt. In his hands he clutched a Heckler and Koch MP 5. On his back he had a huge Bergen rucksack so that he looked like a multicoloured hunchback in his camouflaged uniform.

'Shoot'n'scoot,' the immensely tall SAS colonel shouted above the thunder and flash of the simulator grenades that were exploding on both sides of the running man. 'Hit 'em hard and lethal. Then do a bunk – gildy!'

Next to the colonel and Seal, the little grey-faced civilian clapped his hands together in delight. 'How jolly exciting!' he exclaimed. 'I'm enjoying every minute of this!'

Captain Seal's harshly handsome face lit up in a little smile, but the bright blue eyes remained as wary and cynical as ever. He had never trusted a civilian, whatever their job or rank, for years now.

The SBS trooper skidded to a halt outside the locked door of the training house. Behind him another hooded figure raised a heavy Remington shotgun. He pulled the trigger. There was a tremendous boom. The first man didn't even flinch as a huge charge of high explosive hit the door. The air was full, suddenly, with wooden splinters. As the smoke cleared, the door sagged drunkenly on its hinges.

The first hooded man didn't hesitate, although he was bleeding from a flesh wound in his hand. A 'flash-bang' flew from his good hand. It exploded with an ear-splitting crump. Purple light flashed through the morning gloom. Almost immediately the hooded trooper slammed a salvo from his little machine pistol into the house. Next to Seal, the grey-faced civilian clapped his hands together excitedly, as the tall SAS colonel snapped down the knob of his stop watch. 'Just over thirty seconds. Not bad - for the Special Boat Service.' He gave Seal a mischievous grin.

Seal returned his grin.

'Naturally your chaps will do better when they're fully trained.' He looked down his big nose at the SBS Captain. 'In the SAS we can't be amateurish like your chaps. We train 'em for two years before we even consider 'em for an op. Not like you tip-toe fellahs from Poole.* A couple of weeks in the local municipal baths, another mucking about with boats and then you're off on ops, what.'

'Come, come Arnold,' the little grey civilian said, 'you mustn't put young Seal down like that.' He winked at the tall SAS Colonel. 'I'm sure the SBS chaps do *at least* four weeks training before ops.'

The SAS man winked back and said, 'I'll leave you, now, sir. The place is one hundred percent secure.' He indicated the rusting wire fence of the abandoned RAF airfield. 'The Special Branch boys are patrolling the outer perimeter and my own chaps are doing the same with the inner one.' He touched his right hand to his maroon beret with the winged dagger badge of his regi-

* Headquarters of the Special Boat Service.

ment and turned to go. Behind him his bandy-legged bodyguard armed with a shotgun followed, eyes wary and suspicious.

'Bloody lot of poofters,' Sergeant Hargreaves, Seal's second-in-command, sneered as the SAS men walked to the waiting helicopter. 'I swear one of them brown jobs was using a deodorant.'

Seal smiled and was glad the big Yorkshireman wasn't making his comment in some saloon bar. Then there would have been a right punch-up. The SAS were very touchy about their reputation as tough hombres.

The training exercise was finished now and the men of Seal's Alpha Team slumped in the cropped grass next to the old control tower getting their breath back or puffing silently on a cigarette.

The little grey civilian from MI5 took Seal by the arm as if they had known each other for years and steered him towards the red brick building, shivering a little in the icy wind which hissed across this remote field in Yorkshire. 'I don't know what God was doing when he created Yorkshire,' he said.

'Hell's teeth, that wind must be coming straight from Siberia.'

'It is a little brass monkey, sir,' Seal agreed, wondering again why they had been flown to this place from Poole so mysteriously, earlier that morning. But ever since he had transferred from the Royal Marines to the SBS back in the Eighties, he had become accustomed to strange summons to out of the way places.

The little man gave a sigh of relief as they entered the building, its floor littered with old papers, food trays and a couple of used condoms. 'That's a bit better,' he said and leaning against the dirty wall, he gave Seal a piercing look, as if seeing him for the first time.

He told himself it was hard to believe that the languid young man with the rather too long blond hair had been the first Allied soldier to land behind Saddam Hussein's lines during the Gulf War and that he and the other three men of the Alpha Team had successfully sabotaged most of the Iraqi dictator's oil supplies at Basra; or that he had been engaged in covert ops in Southern

Ireland and sundry other dangerous places ever since.

Seal looked as if he would be more at home in London's clubland, squiring expensive bimbos to expensive nightspots and getting himself written up in the tabloids' gossip columns. But the little grey man from MI5 knew that Seal had already won the DSC twice, had shot his way out of an IRA ambush twice and had received multiple grenade wounds the day he and the Alpha Team had taken out an Islamic Fundamentalist terrorist group off Aden. No, he concluded, Seal was made of the right stuff all right despite that languid upper class pose of his.

Seal stared at the crude drawing of a man with his trousers down on the wall with the legend below it stating, 'It's no use standing on the seat, the crabs in this place jump six feet.'

'Pop art, eh,' the little man said, breaking the heavy silence.

Outside Sergeant Hargreaves was saying in that ponderous Yorkshire fashion of his, 'Never did think nowt o' SAS. Look how they fucked up in the Gulf, getting thesens captured by the wogs and then writing a fucking book about it. *Rubbish!*'

The little man chuckled. 'That's the stuff, esprit de corps. Keeps the chaps on their toes.'

Seal said nothing, he was waiting. He looked at the little man – his grey hair, grey clawlike hands, grey suit. It was almost as if the civilian was already half dead and crumbling away to dust. He sat down heavily on the broken chair and drew the thick overcoat closer, skinny wrinkled face illuminated by a weak yellow ray of the winter sun. He cleared his throat and Seal could hear the thick wheeze of his chest, where the fluid lay.

He waited some more.

Outside Sergeant Hargreaves was saying, 'So I told this SAS bloke, I said to him, "Open yer legs, chum. Nothin'll fall out and even if it does I'll pick 'em up and hand carry 'em back to your wimmin folk in Hereford."* He laughed coarsely. 'Then the

* SAS HQ.

17

cheeky sod upped and punched me. Well, let's say the bugger tried.' He laughed again.

Seal sighed inwardly. The old rivalry between the SBS and the SAS might be good for the esprit de corps, but certainly caused plenty of fist fights.

'It's the Palestinian,' the little grey man said suddenly completely out of the blue.

Seal started. '*Him*!' he exclaimed. 'I thought he was dead.' Everyone in Special Forces knew who the Palestinian was. In the old days, he had been Carlos the Jackal's sidekick. In '75 he had helped in the attack on an Israeli El Al plane at Paris-Orly. Five years later he had instigated the terrorist assault on the US-run radio station 'Radio Free Europe' in Germany's Munich. Three years after that he had bombed the Saudi Arabian Embassy in Athens. In that same year he had attacked the French 'Maison de France' in Berlin. The Palestinian was a terrorist, Seal knew, who worked to order and for any radical government or movement who was prepared to pay good hard German marks to carry out an assignment.

'But I thought he was dead,' Seal repeated when the little civilian didn't react.

The civilian shook his head, as if waking from a heavy sleep. 'So did we. But last week we received information from the Yemenis–'

'The Yemenis,' Seal interrupted. 'I didn't think they'd help *us*.'

The little civilian smiled softly and made the continental gesture of counting money with his thumb and forefinger. 'The Yemenis are broke. They'll do anything for hard currency. Why, only last week they delivered Johannes Weinrich – he worked for Carlos the Jackal, too, for donkey's years – to the Germans for that nice attractive D-Mark of theirs.' The little civilian gave Seal a cynical look. 'So the Yemenis are singing like the proverbial canary and they tell us that the Palestinian is back in business.' He looked to left and right as if he half expected that someone was listening to him. Then he lowered his voice and said in almost a whisper, 'And he's heading this way.'

Seal felt a sudden quickening of his pulse. The only reason that the man from MI5 was revealing this information to him was because Alpha Team was going on ops once more. 'What's the deal?' he asked sharply.

The civilian smiled softly. 'For a chap who was educated at Eton, you do like your Americanisms,' he said. He shrugged. 'No matter, one has to move with the times, I suppose. Well, young Seal, we've got a job for you and your chaps...'

Outside Sergeant Hargreaves was saying, 'I know them SAS blokes are a lot of poofters, but they do feed yer good nosh. I got two fried eggs this morning without asking.'

'The condemned man ate a hearty breakfast,' Corporal 'Dusty' Rhodes announced in his sombre Welsh accent.

Sergeant Hargreaves' reaction was predictable. It was one with which he ended every debate. *'Fook off!'* he said...

Day One

Monday

'Don't yer know there's a war on!'
Slogan of the Phoney War, Winter 1939

Day One

Monday

'Don't yer know there's a war on!'
Slogan of the Phoney War, Winter 1939

Chapter One

The Boeing from Aden-Sanaa hit the tarmac at Luxembourg International with the usual ugly thump. Rubber screeched and metal strained, as the pilot braked hard. The big plane shot down the runway, showering fresh snow to left and right in a crazy white wake. Slowly it began to come to a halt. Now the various tenders and buses started to roll on to the field to deal with the new arrival, their windscreen wipers clicking back and forth furiously, as they tried to deal with the snowstorm.

Now the doors had opened and the first passengers were beginning to file down the steps, shivering in the sudden cold, collars turned up abruptly against the driving snow. Visibility was down to about ten yards now.

A gendarme in the dark blue uniform of the Luxembourg *Gendarmerie* directed them towards immigration. The Boeing had come from a non-EEC country and these days Luxembourg, like the rest of Continental Europe, was concerned with illegal immigrants. After all, one third of the population of the fat little rich country was already foreign; and the good burghers wanted no more of them.

But the snow was too thick even for the wary-eyed gendarme, already concerned about getting back to the warm fug of the airport cafe. So he didn't see the dark-faced slim man in his forties who instead of entering the main airport building turned left and headed for Luxair's cargo port, disappearing into the raging snowstorm almost immediately.

As planned, the little Irishman, seated in his Renault, smoking moodily, shivering now and again with the cold, was waiting for him. He rubbed the window clear, opened it, threw away the *Ducat* he had been smoking and said, 'Joe?'

'Yes, Joe,' the dark-faced man said, his accent only slightly foreign.

Without asking he opened the far door and got in beside the red-faced Irishman, whose breath smelled of whisky although it was only ten in the morning. 'All right, you can take off,' he snapped, like a man accustomed to giving orders – and having them obeyed.

The red-faced Irishman gave him a sour look. 'Bloody wog,' he cursed to himself. Obediently he started up. After all, the boys back home would profit from this deal. The wogs had promised them half a dozen ex-Russian rocket launchers for this one.

'Hamm Cemetery,' the dark-faced man commanded.

'I thought you wanted to go to Lux station–'

'Hamm Cemetery and quick.'

The Irishman shrugged again, but he did as he was ordered, nosing his way into the snow-shrouded traffic, heading towards the US Military Cemetery, where Patton and six thousand men of his World War Two Third Army were buried.

'Did you know old Blood and Guts Patton is buried up there?' the Irishman said, trying to make some sort of conversation with the hard-faced, hook-nosed man.

'Yes, I do. I have never been in Luxembourg in my life before. But I know everything about it. I am well briefed.' His sentences came out in tight-lipped, staccato-like blows from a hammer.

The Irishman lapsed into silence, concentrating on his driving.

Although Hamm Cemetery was only four kilometres away, it took them a good fifteen minutes or more to get there; the roads were very slick with the new snow and traffic was moving slowly. They turned off up the tree-lined drive which led up to the US war cemetery. Automatically, as he had expected, the Palestinian noted that there were no visitors. At this time of the year and in such weather, it was hardly likely that there would be any.

'Halt,' he commanded.

The Irishman looked puzzled, but he obeyed, stopping in front of the imposing gates to the cemetery, with beyond, barely glimpsed, the line after line of crosses, bearing the names of those young men who had been killed violently half a century before. The Irishman shivered. This time it wasn't with the cold. He still had the bog-Irishman's fear of cemeteries.

For what seemed like a long time, the Palestinian didn't move. The Irishman looked at him in the rear view mirror. He was a wog, he told himself, but he looked a tough bastard, a real hard man, in a quiet contained sort of a way. Not a man to force an issue, he thought, but one who would carry it out to the bitter end if he had to.

'All right, you'd better give me the stuff,' the Palestinian said finally.

The Irishman, who had just been about to light another *Ducat*, stopped and reached into the inside pocket of his jacket. 'Here you are,' he said grandly, as if he had achieved something by obtaining the 'stuff.' 'First class ticket from the *Gare de Luxembourg* to Brussels. Fifty thousand francs, that's about–'

'I know how much it is,' the Palestinian interrupted coldly. 'Where are the pounds?'

'Yer, here. Two thousand quid ... and here's the passport. Genuine.' He handed it to the other man.

Quickly the Palestinian flipped through it.

27

Now, suddenly, he seemed to be in a hurry. 'Dr J Hashim, born Poona, 18 December 1950.' He smiled thinly, as he read the words. 'So it must be my birthday today. I'm forty-five.'

The Irishman, unlike most of his countrymen had no sense of humour. He didn't smile at the comment, just looked puzzled.

The Palestinian flipped through it a little further and saw that he had been registered as living in Belgium, in the east cantons to be exact. There was the correct stamp marking the fact, *'Gemeindebüro Meyerode'*. He nodded his head as if pleased.

The Irishman cleared his throat impatiently. It was getting cold inside the Renault without the engine running. He looked pointedly at the Palestinian. The latter saw the look and said, 'Yes, I suppose we'd better be getting to the station.'

The Irishman gave a little smile and reached for the ignition key. It was the last move he ever made. The Palestinian gave him a sudden chop across the side of the carotid artery. His false teeth bulged stupidly from his open mouth. As he reeled, the Palestinian gave him a forehand chop on the back of his head. The Irishman slumped dead over the wheel.

Panting a little, the Palestinian went to work swiftly. Outside the snow whirled in a virtual white-out. As he ripped his nails across the dead man's cheek, blood flowed immediately. Next he zipped open the Irishman's flies. The man's penis welled out. Automatically the Palestinian noted that he wasn't wearing underpants.

Swiftly he searched in his pocket for the photos they had given him in Aden. They were of transvestites, mostly half naked, but very pornographic. They had briefed him in Aden that the Luxembourgers were bourgeois, very moral people. They tolerated prostitution, but didn't like transvestites. Anyone wanting that kind of sex had to take the tarts out into the country. That was why they had picked the cemetery. A lot of that kind did their business here.

He scattered the photos on the back seat, putting on his gloves as he did so. There'd be no prints. He stared around the little car, its windows covered in snow now. Everything seemed all right. Then, as an afterthought, he opened his little Samsonite case and took out his aftershave. He sprinkled the Brut liberally on the man and the seat. 'A lover's quarrel,' he told himself. It'd keep the police busy for a couple of days at least and by then he would be safely where he wanted to be, with no one ever knowing how he got there. They had told him in Aden that you couldn't trust the IRA. That's why the Irishman had to be killed.

He took one last look around and was satisfied. He grabbed his case and opened the door. The storm hit him squarely in the face. He didn't mind. It provided the cover he needed now. He looked at the dead driver with his false teeth bulging out and his penis hanging limply from his flies. *'Shalom Alekhem,'* he said contemptuously. Next moment he was moving swiftly into the storm. A moment later he had disappeared altogether.

Chapter Two

'There she is, sir,' the pilot yelled over the intercom, as the helicopter started to circle over the grey-green waves, 'the pride of UK Oil... The *Margaret Thatcher*.'

Baron von Klarsfeld nodded his understanding. The snow had now given way to a thin bitter rain, which streamed down the glass of the cockpit like cold tears. All the same he could see the rig all right, as it appeared to bob up and down in the turbulence. 'The Iron Lady, we call her,' the pilot added. 'You know why, sir.'

Baron von Klarsfeld's expression did not change. He had no sense for small talk or humour. 'Send the signal, Hermann,' he commanded, 'or they'll probably start shooting at us down there. The English are a thuggish lot.'

'Yessir.' Obediently the pilot began to send UK Oil's code word with his signal lamp, while the Baron, muffled up in his expensive green *Loden* coat, complete with fur collar, studied the rig through his binoculars.

It was an impressive-looking structure. Twenty thousand tons of steel towering four hundred feet above the North Sea. Red warning lights flickered the length of its top deck, littered with steel piping – forty thousand feet of it, the Baron knew, laid out in thirty foot sections. It irritated him to have to use these archaic English measurements, but the English refused obstinately to employ the metric section. As he had often remarked to his friends on the Frankfurt *Boerse:* 'The English are stubborn, spiteful and in terminal senility. They never will change their ways.'

He ran his field glasses, the same ones he used for hunting bear in the Carpathians at the weekend, that is when he wasn't jetting to his yacht at Port de France, the length of the derrick floor. The rig's centre of activity sparkled with high power lights, illuminating the rotary table.

It was here that the table turned the drill pipe which at that very moment was digging deep into the seabed, some six hundred feet below. It could go on for a further 9,000 feet. But naturally, UK Oil hoped to strike oil long before that. Von Klarsfeld gave a pudgy grin. If the company didn't, they'd be out of business pretty damn quick.

'See those in the white hats, sir,' the pilot shouted, 'they're soon finishing their tour. You can see that by the slow way they're working.' He grinned. 'They're saving up their strength for the whores in Hull and Grimsby.'

'I wish you wouldn't use that coarse language,' von Klarsfeld said primly. 'You're not a *Bundeswehr* jet jockey now, you know.'

'No sir. Sorry, sir,' the pilot answered swiftly. Flying jobs were hard to come by in civvie street and he didn't want to lose this one. To himself, however, he said, 'Go and piss in yer boot, arse-with-ears.' Von Klarsfeld lowered his glasses and flashed a look at his Rolex. It was the eighteenth. Today the men below would be finishing their tour and heading for Bridlington. 'Who's in charge of the new tour tonight, Hermann?' he asked.

'Red Ross, sir,' the pilot answered. 'Big bastard. Very tough. Hates Germans, the shit.'

For once Baron von Klarsfeld didn't object to the pilot's strong language. It was justified. He knew that the Englishman Ross was one of the most experienced pushers* in the business. If anyone could get the 'Margaret Thatcher' to produce oil after a disappointing series of dry holes, it would be the big flaming-haired Yorkshireman, with his face that looked as if it had been carved out of granite.

He absorbed the news as the pilot circled the helicopter once more then he said, 'All right, let's get back to base. There's a board meeting in London this afternoon.'

'Jawohl, Herr Baron,' the pilot snapped, as if he were still back in the Bundeswehr, addressing some superior officer. To himself he said, 'Arseholes of the world unite. The fat cats are going to get their snouts in the money trough again.'

Von Klarsfeld settled himself more com-

* Roughly – foreman.

34

fortably in his seat, his mind already occupied by other things. Behind them the great rig slipped away into the gloom. It was a symbol of the real feebleness of man, dwarfed by the enormous cruel expanse of the green sea. Yet at the same it was a symbol of the strength of human will and determination, man's power to bend nature to his own devices.

Germany, the Baron told himself, was totally dependent on outside sources for its oil and natural gas. Admittedly there was some native oil around Karlsruhe, but it didn't amount to much. As of the moment, Germany's total oil and natural gas came from the new GUS states, the Middle East and in particular Saudi Arabia. All these sources were highly vulnerable. What the New Germany wanted, the Baron knew, was a secure source, in its own backyard, which could be protected by the German *Bundesmarine,* if necessary.

That was why the consortium he led needed to take over UK oil. There was plenty of oil down there, their own geologists had assured them of that. All that was needed to find it was time and money. He smiled softly, the unpleasant smile of a predatory. And UK Oil had neither.

Pleased with himself he took out a cigar and lit it. He knew that it was forbidden to smoke in the helicopter. But what the hell, he thought. After all he owned the damned thing...

'Red' Ross picked up the phone and dialled the central London number. He asked for the major and the very posh receptionist at the other end said, 'Will you hold, sir?' Without waiting for his answer there was a burst of music which Red Ross now knew was, 'some eyetie called bloody Viveldi', as he explained it to his mates in the pub.

As he waited Red Ross stared at the ugly grey-green wash of the North Sea. A couple of fishing boats were leaving the harbour, bound for the outer sea. Probably filled with mugs from the West Riding who thought they could catch anything but cold off the Head. In the corridor a cleaner, with a cigarette dangling from her bottom lip was hoovering the carpet so fiercely that it seemed that she might want to wear a hole in it.

'Red.' It was the Major, as he was known throughout the oil business, where all the field workers had some sort of nickname or other.

'Yes, Major, me,' Red Ross said in a thick East Yorkshire accent. 'Trouble.'

'What's it this time, Red?' the Major asked and the concern was obvious in his voice. Red knew why. The money was running out fast and they needed to strike oil soon at the *Margaret Thatcher,* if they wanted to get any further credit from the finance boys.

'I'm six bodies short on the new tour. Once those blokes get their pay, they're off to the tarts and boozers. I'm looking for fresh bodies though, but I'm pressed.' He sighed wearily. 'I don't know, people these days, a bit o' money and they vanish, get a dose, get married, perhaps sign up with some other company for more pay.'

'So it's more pay again,' Major Honor MC said almost sadly. 'Always bloody money.' He raised his voice. 'All right, Red, this is what you do. Give the roughnecks another tenner and the roustabouts perhaps another fifteen pounds.'

'Yes Major. Will do. But there's something wrong with the blokes we hire, sir. A couple of years back they were fighting to get jobs on the rigs, in particular the *Margaret Thatcher*. Now they all seem so bolshy. The bastards walk around the rig as if they might rupture themsens if you asked 'em to pick up a bloody wrench. You know what, Major, I think we've got a bloody lemon on board.'

'A lemon?'

'Yessir.' Through the hotel's big picture window he could see the helicopter heading south to London and he didn't need a crystal ball to know whose it was. It belonged to that bloody German Baron, spying on the rig again. 'Yessir,' he repeated as the noise of the chopper started to die away. 'Somebody on the rig is getting to the shifts. My guess is that we've got a union man aboard.'

'Holy Christ!' the Major moaned. 'That too.'

For the first time since Red Ross had known the Major, and that had been a long time ago in another country, he noted the despair in his boss's voice. He told himself that after two years of disappointment after disappointment, Major Justin Honor, MC was about at the end of his tether.

Chapter Three

Justin Honor had been an eighteen-year-old at Eton when the Korean War had broken out. He had volunteered for his father's old regiment, the Glosters, immediately and had been commissioned almost at once. 'It's only a little war,' they had chortled, old hands and the new boys, as they had sailed for the Far East, 'but it's the only war we've got.'

In the event it turned out to be a damn big war for the Glosters. On the Hook Ridge the eight hundred-odd of them had fought twenty thousand or more Chinese, racing towards them, bugles blaring, flags flying and all shrieking as if they were high on drugs or drink. They had mowed them down in their hundreds but still they had kept on coming. His C.O. and most of the surviving officers had been forced to surrender to face months, even years, in captivity. He, however, had been able to escape with that was left of his platoon. For days they had wandered, every man's hand against them, behind Chinese lines, but finally the exhausted men had made it and at the tender age of eighteen he found himself the proud possessor of the Military Cross.

For a while he had considered staying in the Army, but the thought of years of square bashing and bull had appalled him. Instead he had gone into the rough-and-tumble of the oil business, an ex-major at twenty-two. He had travelled the world, working on rigs as an ordinary hand, till finally he had landed in the head office of an American oil company based in London with the rank of second vice-president. Then on June 22nd, 1971 his world changed dramatically. On that day the government announced that bids were being invited for the new fields which had been discovered off Britain's east coast.

He had told his secretary he was going out for a little breath of air, although it was drizzling outside. For an hour and half he had walked the streets aimlessly, wondering what he should do. After all, he was risking a good job. He had kids at prep school and his wife would take unkindly to the loss of the luxuries she had become accustomed to. But in the end he had gone into a newsagent's shop, bought some cheap note paper and a batch of envelopes and had scribbled his bid on the paper with the newsagent's biro. Soaked by now, he had taken a taxi and had deposited his bid at 1247 Thames House South, Millbank. Then he had gone back to his office, surprising his secretary a little by his bedraggled appearance, and had sat at his desk, as if nothing had happened.

One month later he had found himself in possession of one hundred square miles of seabed some forty miles off the Yorkshire coast and without a job. The American bosses back in Texas had fired him immediately when they had found out he had made a successful bid when they had failed. UK Oil had been born.

Things had gone well for him thereafter. The first rig had started to produce within eighteen months. Six months after that, he had been able to pay off his debts to the city bankers and his second rig was producing at a profit.

The years went by and as his American friends always said, 'You're living high on the hog, Justin,' which he was. But by the late Eighties the oil had started to run out and the company, UK Oil, had started to close rigs, wondering how the devil they were going to get rid of the steel and concrete monsters.

In 1990 he had been given another chance. His geologists had found another area of the North Sea with the same oil-bearing sedimentary rock, which had started the 'Great North Sea Oil Rush', as the papers had proclaimed it all those years before.

But this time his luck appeared to have run out. Twice this winter the sides of the *Margaret Thatcher's* boring hole had caved in, causing 'fishes': the wearisome business of stopping the whole operation and clearing up the nasty mess. Then they had had a 'twist-off' – a major drilling mishap –

with the drilling string broken far below the surface, creating an even more difficult 'fish'. And the money provided by the American-German consortium, headed by Baron von Klarsfeld was draining away rapidly, some fifty thousand pounds a day.

Now it seemed he had a union man on the right, something which had not happened before. That would have the Americans reaching for their little pink pills and Baron von Klarsfeld, used to the tame German industrial unions, wouldn't be too happy either.

'Christ!' Major Honor exclaimed, looking at the bitter rain streaming down the window of his office. 'Where will I get the money from now?'

But there was no answer to that over-whelming question.

Chapter Four

'*Illegals*,' Sergeant Hargreaves said, closing the top secret identification book, as the skimmer rocked back and forth on the waves. 'Not registered at Lloyds under that name and specifications.'

Seal eyed the little coaster in the afternoon gloom for a few moments longer. The Alpha Team had been allotted this stretch of the North Sea to check, while other SBS teams did the same further south. The whole service was now operational, together with MI5, Special Branch and the like. The SAS at Hereford were on stand by, too. It was almost like wartime, trying to seal off the whole country on account of one single terrorist, but then the Palestinian was something very special. 'All right,' he snapped to Cox at the rudder, his mind made up, 'let's go and check it out.'

At his side Sergeant Hargreaves sneered,

'The whole bloody North Sea full of bleeding drug pushers, illegal immigrants and fucking Spaniards nobbling all our fucking fish. What a world!'

'What a world indeed, Hargreaves, but it's the only one we've got–' His words ended in a gulp and he grabbed for support as the skimmer surged forward at full speed, seeming to slide over the waves, half out of the water.

At forty knots an hour, the little craft, which had been designed specially for the SBS, for it could move on land as well as on water, ideal for infiltration exercise, closed the distance to the old tub rapidly. Now she loomed up in front of them, all peeling paintwork and rust, chugging along at ten knots an hour, a flag which Seal couldn't identify hanging limply at her bow.

They were spotted. Seal could see a small figure on the bridge pointing in their direction to another figure, and even by their stance, he could tell the two men were alarmed. 'We're on to something, Hargreaves,' he yelled, the wind whipping the words out of his mouth, as on the coaster a klaxon started to sound the alarm. 'Ready for anything.'

'Too bloody true,' Hargreaves snorted almost angrily. 'Haven't shot anybody since the Gulf. I'm getting out of practice.' He pulled the big American automatic from beneath his blouse and clicked off the safety threateningly. Next to him, Seal did the same. These days, dope runners, illegals and the rest of the scum plying their trade in British waters wouldn't think twice about murdering even policemen, weighing them down with something and slinging the bodies over the side. One had to be prepared for anything.

The first burst of slugs hit the water just feet ahead of them. The sea rose in angry spurts. Next to Seal, Sergeant Hargreaves cursed, 'Sod this for a game of soldiers.' Balancing himself the best he could, he gripped his big automatic in both hands and loosed off a volley. The man who had fired at them threw up his arms, as if praying to heaven for help. There was none forthcoming. Next instant he slumped over the rail and slithered into the water.

At the rudder, Cox zigzagged the skimmer wildly, as another of the coaster's crew opened up with an Uzi.

Bullets hissed into the water all around them. Grimly Seal prayed their engine wouldn't be hit. Then they'd really be for the chop.

'Take her portside, Cox!' he yelled above the roar of the speeding engine.

'Sir,' Cox yelled back. He spun the skimmer round effortlessly. The man with the Uzi vanished rapidly, as the skimmer sped into the lee of the coaster. Now its rusty peeling sides towered above them like a steel cliff.

'Grapnel, Higgins!' Seal yelled.

Higgins, the fourth member of the Alpha Team, big and burly and 'built like a brick shithouse', as Hargreaves was wont to describe him in that no-nonsense manner of his, needed no urging. He knew exactly what to do. He picked up the grapnel pistol and fired it. The steel grapnel shot out from the muzzle. Behind it the super strength nylon cord snaked upwards. The grapnel struck metal with a satisfying clang.

Seal shot a look upwards. Faintly he could hear feet running along the deck, but so far it appeared that no one had spotted the grapnel. He made his decision. 'You hold her Cox,' he ordered. 'We're going up.'

'Ay,' Sergeant Hargreaves said almost happily, a grin on his craggy red face. 'We're gonna sort the buggers out and if there's any trouble,' he flourished the automatic, 'yours truly will only be too glad to banjo the buggers.' With that he started to scale the nylon ladder, climbing upwards at an amazing speed for such a big man. Seal followed.

Hargreaves swung himself low over the rail and they crouched on their haunches, pistols at the ready. The sound of running feet and shouts grew closer. Seal guessed they had been spotted or someone was coming to check where the skimmer was.

A dark-faced man in a tattered seaman's uniform came running round the edge of the superstructure. He was carrying an Uzi machine pistol. He skidded to a halt when he saw the three intruders crouched. He raised the Uzi. Higgins didn't give him a chance to use it. He fired the pump shotgun. The seaman screamed high and hysterical like a woman. His face disappeared in a gory red welter. Next moment it seemed to be slithering to his chest like melting sealing wax. An instant later he slammed down to the deck, dead or unconscious.

'Come on,' Seal urged, 'move it!'

They needed no urging. They all knew that the man who hesitates in battle will soon be a dead man. Moving targets were harder to hit. They doubled forward, crouched low, weapons at the ready. Out of the portholes to their right, dark faces, frightened and bulging-eyed, peered out at them.

'Paki-runner,' Hargreaves commented as they ran on.

Seal didn't answer. He was saving his breath. Somehow he didn't think the crew of the coaster would be risking this lethal fire fight just to run in some illegal immigrants from Pakistan. It wouldn't be worth their lives at a thousand pounds a head.

He swung round the edge of the bridge. A big bluff man with a beard was standing there, as if waiting for them, revolver in hand. *'Was wollt Ihr Scheisshund?'* he bellowed in fury.

'Bloody Hermanns as well as Pakis,' Hargreaves yelled angrily.

The German aimed. Hargreaves didn't give him a chance. He fired first. The big man grunted with pain. The revolver fell from his hand and he went down on one knee, clutching it, the blood jetting from the wound in a scarlet arc.

Seal ran to him. He pressed the muzzle of his pistol, knuckle white as he curled it around the trigger. 'OK, *Herr Kapitan,*' he ordered in German, *'jetzt genug. Mach' kein Theater. Aufgeben.'*

'Schon gut,' the wounded captain groaned, and then in English. 'No shooting more.'

Five minutes later Hargreaves and Higgins had rounded up the motley crew and disarmed them. Now they squatted on the wet deck, hands above their heads in the wet drizzle, glaring sullenly at Hargreaves and Higgins – something which didn't faze those two guys one bit – while Seal questioned the captain.

'All right, so you are carrying Pakistanis from Holland for illegal entry,' Seal said patiently, while the German captain stared at the blood still squirting from his wounded leg, as if he couldn't believe that this was happening to him. 'But you wouldn't have fired at us just on account of some illegal immigrants. So what's the deal?' He stared hard at the wounded man.

'You must help me,' the Captain moaned. 'I bleed to death.'

'Yes, you will,' Seal answered calmly. 'In fact, I will ensure that that happens if you don't tell me why you took such a risk.' As if to emphasize just what he said, Seal kicked the wounded captain's leg. More blood spurted from the wound in a ugly black gob and splattered across the dirty deck. The Captain looked at it aghast. *'Hast du kapiert?'* Seal added harshly.

'Yes, yes,' the German said hurriedly. 'I understand.'

'Well, then speak up and we'll get you back to Hull, to the hospital there.'

'But if I speak, they will kill me,' the German moaned.

Seal shrugged carelessly. 'So what. You'll die the other way then. At least, you'll have a chance if you tell me what's going on.'

The Captain swallowed hard, then with tears of self-pity running down his weathered face, he began. 'Semtex,' he said. 'I was paid to take semtex...'

Hargreaves flashed Higgins a glance. It said, 'Christ almighty, we've struck paydirt.'

Chapter Five

The boardroom of UK Oil was thick and blue with the smoke of expensive cigars. The elegant Regency table, which the company secretaries had laid out so carefully before the meeting with flowers and the like, was now littered with overflowing ashtrays, empty bottles of Perrier water and screwed-up stubs of paper and calculations.

They had arrived in cool expectation, not realising what was waiting for them. While von Klarsfeld, looking very smug and superior, smoked his cigar in silence, Trix, the fat little banker from Houston, had reeled off one unpleasant statistic after another, all the while waving his fat cigar in Major Honor's direction, as if he wished he could grind its burning tip out in the Britisher's fading blue eyes.

'So,' he concluded in the end, 'UK Oil is just about broke and there's no further possibility of raising any further money in Houston. We're having troubles enough of our own in the States. Christ, that Clinton.' He sighed like a sorely troubled man, mopped his damp brow with a floral handkerchief and looked at the German representative, von Klarsfeld, significantly.

Von Klarsfeld ignored the look. His pudgy face as arrogant as ever, he continued to puff his cigar silently.

Outside it had begun to snow again and the windows were beginning to steam up. Major Honor told himself that the mood of the boardroom was pretty much the same. It was time for him to say something.

Slowly he rose to his feet. They looked at him. As an afterthought he took a sip of Perrier, though he would have dearly loved to have had a double scotch instead. He forced a smile. 'All of us have been through crises like this before. That's the nature of the oil business.'

Trix nodded his agreement and muttered, 'You can say that again, brother.'

Von Klarsfeld continued to puff at his cigar.

'We've been at it a long time now, as you all know. So far to no advantage save for those kinds of fish which prefer to copulate in very deep holes.'

There was some weak laughter and von Klarsfeld broke his silence to comment with obvious contempt, 'Ah, that celebrated English humour. We in Germany prefer to call it *Galgenhumor*. I translate for you, gentlemen, "gallows humour".'

Honor could have strangled him. But von Klarsfeld was typical. Since Germany's reunification five years before, there were a lot like him, ready to throw their weight around. Soon they would saying that Chamberlain started the war.

Honor forced a smile all the same. 'Gentlemen,' he continued, 'it is often said that if you owe a bank a pound, *you're* in trouble, but if you owe it a million pounds, *the bank's* in trouble.' He grinned at Trix and then at von Klarsfeld. 'Our bankers must be really in big trouble, because we owe them *twenty* million.'

That caused a real laugh and a very fruity English voice said, 'That's telling 'em, Justin.'

Trix laughed and mopped his brow again, while suddenly von Klarsfeld lost his look of arrogance. Abruptly he realized that his masters at the Dresdner, Deutsche and Commerz Banks wouldn't be too happy when they heard that he had been the one who had talked them into helping to fund the original loan to UK Oil.

'So what's to be done?' Honor spread out his hands, as if appealing to them.

There were mumbles and muttered undertones of 'you tell us, old chap' and 'no good throwing good money after bad'.

Honor ignored the comments. Iron in his voice, he snapped, 'We've just got to bash on. We'll find oil I am absolutely sure of that. In fact I'm going to take over the rig myself.'

There was a gasp and Honor felt that old thrill of danger, the same kind he had experienced on the Hook when Lance Corporal Stevens had thrown down his bren and moaned, as the Chinese hordes got ever closer, 'Let's jack it frigging well in, sir. We don't stand a chance in frigging hell against all them Chinks.' He had slapped Stevens across the face in rage and, seizing the bren, had tucked that satisfying butt into his shoulder and had blazed away at the attackers. That had stopped them for a while. That same night they had commenced their successful retreat.

'What did you say, Major?' the man from Houston had said.

'I said I'm going to take over *Margaret Thatcher* myself. I know the money market has no confidence in me and my leadership. Well,' Honor said defiantly, 'it's going to have confidence in me and my leadership for one more week. If I don't bring in oil by seven days from now, you can have UK Oil.' He looked pointedly at Baron von Klarsfeld, who he suspected was behind this emergency meeting of the board.

The German actually blushed with embarrassment.

Five minutes later Honor was sipping his large whisky and soda gratefully, as Hilary, his secretary, looked down at him, a worried look on her face, fussing him with, 'Won't you have a sandwich, sir?' and, 'Can't I go out and get you something from

61

the coffee shop?'

He patted her hand and said, 'Don't fuss about me like a mother hen, dear Hilary.' He knew she would have gone to bed with him like a shot. She was utterly devoted to him. What would old Lance Corporal Stevens, long dead in Korea, have said if he had known that his granddaughter all of twenty-two, was utterly devoted to a sixty-three year old, whom he had once described as, 'that toffee-nosed young git, who thinks he's lord muck just cos he's got one pip on his shoulder. Christ, I've shat officers like 'im before today.'

'Well, I've done it, Hilary,' he said, draining his glass and rising stiffly to his feet. He stared at the large white flakes hitting the window of his office like white tracer. 'There's no turning back now.'

'You will be careful, sir,' Hilary said, her lush young body so close that he was tempted to seize her. It was two years now since he had a woman. His second wife had left him when he told her he was going to sink all their remaining money into the *Margaret Thatcher.*

He resisted the impulse and laughed, touching her pretty hand lightly and saying, 'There's a French expression which sums up my present situation.'

'What's that, sir?' she asked, colouring because she had guessed what had just gone through his mind.

'*Marcher ou crever.*'

'What does it mean?'

He looked at her hard. 'March or die...'

Chapter Six

'Hashim.'

The Palestinian awoke at once. Without even a gasp of surprise, his hand darted under the pillow. Outside the traffic was muted. Brussels was going to sleep. Then he lowered the automatic slowly. There was no need for fear. It was the girl. Poised at the door, he could see her naked body through the transparent lace of her nightdress in the light that came from the flat's corridor.

'What do you wish?' he asked in his careful French.

Monique giggled and answered, *'You!'*

He frowned. He didn't like women, in particular he didn't like mixing them with business. All the same, he needed her. She was to help him on the next stage of his journey. But like most of these European left-wing female intellectuals, who supported the cause, she wanted romance as well as conspiracy. Perhaps, he told himself, the two went together for these silly European females. He pushed the pistol beneath his pillow and moved over. 'Come,' he commanded.

She needed no urging. She slipped into the bed, threw her bare arms around his neck and gave him a long, open-mouthed girl's kiss. He wrinkled his nose in disgust. She smelled of drink and women's sex. He feigned breathlessness, pushing her away a little. 'Please M'lle Monique, you're choking me.'

She plumped down on the bed carelessly, legs spread to reveal the dark triangle of pubic hair, her full breasts straining through the thin material of her nightdress. She grinned lasciviously. 'I'd love to. I'd love to do anything *you* want, however perverted. You know you're really beautiful – like a thin shaven Carlos.'

He restrained a sigh. That was what it was all about with these European women lefties. They didn't want a revolution. No, they just wanted to go to bed with the revolutionaries. He flashed a glance at his watch. It was nearly midnight and he was tired; it had been a long day. All the same he knew he had to fuck her. It could be her task to get him safely from Brussels to the port of Zeebrugge tomorrow. 'Come on then,' he said.

She didn't hesitate. Eagerly, as if she couldn't get her hands on him soon enough. She threw off his cover with a sigh of delight. His long naked body, heavy with solid muscle around the shoulder, matted with thick dark hair from chest to loins. *'Wow!'* she exclaimed. 'And that thing – the size of it.' She reached out a hand for his penis as if she were a little afraid of it and squeezed it.

He willed himself to harden immediately, as he had been trained to do so long ago in Moscow, when he had attended the KGB sex course. It was a matter of muscular control, not lust. He didn't feel a thing for her.

He ran the tips of his fingers down the small of her back, underneath her gown right to the split between the buttocks. She shivered with delight. 'Anything, you want,' she whispered in a shaky voice.

He thrust up her gown, pulled it over her head and then ran his wet lips across the girl's nipples. She closed her eyes, face screwed up as if she couldn't stand the pleasure. Her nipples hardened immediately, becoming thick and dun. Automatically she took her right breast and fed it more into his mouth like a fond mother feeding a beloved baby. He sucked the nipples hard. Her face glistened with sweat and her breath start to come in savage little gasps.

His right hand slipped between her legs. She was already wet. Bitch, he told himself, a randy little bitch. Like an animal on heat. They have no shame these European women.

He started to play with her as she moaned and writhed, lips slack and wet, her mouth gaping, her face a sudden ugly red. 'Oh, good ... oh, good,' she kept saying with boring regularity.

He looked at her stupid face with contempt. Suddenly he stopped. 'Take it in your mouth,' he commanded, 'and suck it hard.'

Blindly, still sobbing for breath, she bent to his loins. She took it in her mouth, tongue curling wetly about the stem.

'More,' he ordered sternly, 'more, I say. Or there'll be trouble for you, woman.'

She mumbled something and did as he commanded.

He put his hands behind his head and stared down at her as she sucked and licked at his loins. Suddenly he found he was enjoying himself. He knew it was because he was in total command. He knew, too, that he could make the woman do anything, the grossest of perversions and she would do it to please him. He ordered himself to feel no pleasure yet. He would have to satisfy her first, perhaps more than once, then he could climax. That's what they had taught him in Moscow back in the days when he had been young and idealistic, passionate in his belief in the cause. Now he just hated the West and acted only if he were paid to do so.

She looked up, her lips swollen and wet with saliva.

'Please ... please do it to me,' she quavered. 'Oh, please ... I need it now.' Her stupid face was full of pleading.

'All right,' he snapped, completely in charge. 'On your stomach.'

She hesitated. 'Will it hurt?' she asked.

'Do as you are told, woman!' he thundered.

Hurriedly she turned and lay on her stomach, plump buttocks thrust upwards.

He grinned sadistically. Slowly, very slowly, savouring the moment, he parted her legs. He hovered above her. Carefully he inserted his organ. Her buttocks trembled. She was liking it already, he told himself. They always protested, but in the end they couldn't get enough of it. He thrust a little deeper. She yelped. He grinned, eyes cruel and determined. He thrust even deeper. 'Ouch.' She cried and then he let her have all of it, putting his hand over her mouth to muffle her cries.

'Come on, bitch,' he grunted, pumping his loins back and forth, the sweat pouring down his face, 'now enjoy it'

It was an hour later. She lay in his arms absolutely exhausted, muttering at periodic intervals just how much she loved him and how 'wonderful' he had been to her. No man had ever made love to her like that before. He, for his part, lay smoking moodily and staring at the ceiling. He still had not ejaculated. His training had seen to that. He could take her another half a dozen times and still be in control of himself, if he wished. But he told himself that by now she'd had enough. She'd drift off to sleep soon and leave him in peace.

But he was wrong. Slowly she began to kiss him again. Her hand reached out and took his organ, as if it were something very precious. She cupped it in her hand and with her breath coming faster once more, she whispered into his ear what she would like to do for him. He nodded. He made his breath come faster, as if she had excited him above measure. She ran her face the length of his lean body, showering it with feathery little kisses. Her mane of long blonde hair settled around his loins hiding them. He made himself give a couple of sighs of fake passion. When he thought that she had excited herself enough, he flung her over on her back and thrust open her legs. Like the trained stallion he was, he plunged himself into her as she writhed back and forth in uncontrolled passion, the beads of sweat pouring down her face, giving off little moans. This time he allowed himself to climax inside her. Minutes later she was fast asleep on the rumpled sheet, snoring softly, with her mouth open.

He looked down at her sweat-lathered face surrounded by the matted hair contemptuously. 'Whore,' he whispered. 'If it's boy call it Hashim—'

He stopped short. A car had braked outside, disturbing the night silence. There was the sound of whispered voices. A moment later another car drew up. More whispered conversation. He was wide awake in a flash. He sensed danger in the air. Was it something to do with the whore? Or had the authorities rumbled him already?

Noiselessly he got out of the bed. Naked he padded to the window, careful to keep in the shadows. He pulled the edge of the curtain to one side. There were two cars parked under the streetlight at the opposite side. Further up the road at the corner there were two policemen in uniform, clad in bulky overcoats. He knew why immediately. They were wearing body armour beneath them. He had been rumbled.

Hashim wasted no more time. He dressed silently, slipping his shoes in his pockets. Carefully so as not to disturb the girl, he slipped his automatic from beneath the rumpled pillow. He'd have to find his way to Zeebrugge without her. He tiptoed into the living room. The drinks were still on the table next to her handbag. He picked it up and took out her car keys. The car was in the underground garage beneath the block of flats. As an afterthought he took the wad of franc notes from her purse. You never know, he told himself, as he stuffed them into his inside pocket. Money was power, too.

He paused and thought for a moment. They had not penetrated the block yet. Even if they had, it wouldn't have mattered because the lift went straight down to the underground garage. But where was the key to the place? He walked swiftly from the darkened living room to the kitchen, also in darkness, though there was some light coming in from the streetlight outside.

He sniffed. Revolutionary she might be, but the girl was bourgeois all the same, typical Belgian middle class. His nose wrinkled in contempt at the home-made egg warmers, embroidered with hearts and flowers, the knives, all in their special places, the chocolate box Victorian picture of a woman and child on the wall. Absolute kitsch, he told himself. Then he spotted what he wanted – the keyboard – each key labelled in a careful hand. Hastily he seized the garage key.

He left, locking the door of the apartment behind him and threw the key down the rubbish chute. That'd keep them busy for a few minutes when they rushed the apartment. He got into the lift. Hastily he unscrewed the roof light. He would descend in darkness. He hoped the lift wouldn't make too much noise.

It didn't. He descended into the freezing garage almost noiselessly. He went to the door grill and peered out into a side street. No one there, it seemed. Carefully he unlocked it and pushed the grill back. He went to her car. He knew which one it was because she had picked him up in it from the Gare du Nord. It was a *deux chevaux,* of course. That was the rickety type of car her sort always drove. The 'Greens' probably thought it was 'eco-sound', as they called such things. One thing was for sure, the 2CV was light, ideal for what he had to do now.

He put it into neutral and then slowly he started to push it towards the garage door. He didn't want to start up. That might alert the people at the front of the block. There was a slight slope, but he managed it. Now the dark side street lay before him. It had started to snow again. The flakes were coming down quite thickly. All the same he was grateful. The snow would give him the cover he needed. It would also deaden any sound the little Citroën's wheels might make. He pushed the car outside. Nothing stirred.

He got behind the wheel, took the brake off and with one foot outside the door gave it a good shove. The Citroën started to roll slowly forward down the slope. Behind him in the house, he could hear the sound of heavy boots stamping across the *parterre*. That would be the cops, who would have to be present when they broke into the flat. It was standard operating procedure. He grinned. They were in for a surprise. A drunken woman, with sperm still trickling down the inside of her naked thighs.

The Citroën started to move more rapidly. Up ahead loomed the main road. Cars were still moving up and down it. He judged it safe to start the motor. He turned the key. The motor sprang to life immediately. He cast a look in the rear-view mirror. Nothing! He grinned. He had done it again.

The girl would obviously talk in due course. These revolutionary heroes of the middle class always did. But by then he hoped to have ditched the car. He turned on the lights and swung into the traffic, his windscreen wipers ticking back and forth as the snow thickened. Five minutes later the Palestinian was on his way past the three silver balls of the atomium westwards, heading for his date with destiny.

Day Two

Tuesday

'The whole of the warring nations are engaged, not only soldiers, but the entire population, men, women and children. The fronts are everywhere. The trenches are dug in the towns and streets. Every village is fortified. The front line runs through the factories. The workers are soldiers with different weapons, but the same courage.'

Winston Churchill, Summer 1940

Chapter One

'Red' Ross's tour had its first 'fish' exactly at dawn. Outside it was snowing again, large white flakes. The cold ate into the bones of the men working on the platform. As the old shift moved stiffly about their tasks, like a collection of ancient ghosts, they told themselves they were in for a 'right old blizzard' before the day was out. The 'fish', however, beat the storm to it.

Just after seven when the cooks were serving the first steak and chips (black pudding optional) of the day and they would continue serving the same meal every hour thereafter, the rotary started to spin faster and faster. The green luminous hands of the torque recorder, the weight indicator and the various mud pressure dials began to slacken off alarmingly. The head driller reacted swiftly enough. He braked the console. Then he shouted a warning.

The crew knew that 'Red' Ross would hit the ceiling when he found out. He had a short fuse at the best of times. So they mumbled together for a while as the snowflakes came drifting down and decided to give it another couple of turns. To no avail. It was a 'fish' all right. There was no denying that.

'Christ All-Frigging-Mighty!' Ross exploded when they told him. 'Doesn't nowt ever go frigging right on the *Margaret Thatcher*?' Then the big red-haired boss pulled himself together and set about finding what had happened. In the end, after checking the pre-dawn records, he announced, 'All right, lads, we've got a cave-in. The pipe's stuck in a bad place. We've got a deviated hole. All the old shift can get some kip. The new boy'll take care of this particular sod.'

All that morning 'Red' Ross directed operations personally. Cupping his big chapped hands around his mouth he roared against the mounting force of the storm and had the Bowen overshot lowered into place, while far below the grey-green sea rose and sank, each wave seemingly larger than the last. He hoped with the overshot they would be able to engage the broken section of piping and draw it out.

In the end, with the cold sea spray running down their wind-reddened faces, their overalls thick with grey mud, the shift was forced to give up. The Bowen was not gripping. Red Ross controlled himself with difficulty. Half the shift was almost over and they had not drilled a foot of damned rock.

'All right, lads,' he yelled above the howl of the wind, 'let's run a washpipe down and see if we can free the bugger with that.'

There was a collective groan from the crewmen. The washpipe, with which Red hoped to wash out the broken part, involved a lot of back breaking work. Reluctantly, their cracked bruised hands stiff with cold, they started to break out the new gear, hating what was to come.

The snowy afternoon passed in leaden, dogged, brutal hard work. The elements didn't help either. Time and time again there were bitter flurries of snow that created a white-out in an instant, and which whipped frozen spray across their crimson faces.

Tempers started to fray. A roustabout dropped a wrench on his foot and cursed his mate viciously and at length, till it seemed they might stop work and begin a fist-fight. The cooks brought up tea and the men cursed them for serving 'lukewarm gnat's piss'. The cooks fled. Then the radio operator, Jacko Simpson, reported that the chopper which brought in the daily supplies and mail was delayed. Perhaps it might not even make the rig this day due to bad weather. That news was received with boos and threats of doing something anatomically impossible to the radio operator. He fled, too.

Then they lost the overshot and Red Ross's temper flared up dramatically. 'Listen you bunch of birdbrains, I'm going to the heads to take a piss. But when I come back, I'll expect you bastards to have recovered the overshot – or else.' He clenched two fists like small steam shovels and departed, fumbling with the flies of his mud-stained overalls.

When he returned half an hour later, deliberately having taken his time in the latrine, they had recovered the overshot. But by now their mood had changed from open anger at their lot and the job to a sullen glowering resentment. They no longer spoke to one other. Instead they carried out their tasks with brisk nods of their heads or gestures. So they worked without any attempt to break the taut brooding silence and Red Ross realised that there was trouble brewing.

They were making progress, he could see that as he stood there chewing tobacco, a habit he had picked up when it had still been forbidden to smoke on rigs, but he knew that something was going to give – and give soon...

It happened just after midday. On the elevators, one of the shift miscalculated and dropped one of the elevators just in front of a floorman with a tremendous crash. The startled floorman jumped back and then shouted, hands cupped around his mouth against the howling, wind 'What the bloody hell do you think yer doing, yer long streak of piss.'

Red Ross shouted too, 'Why can't yer do yer frigging job properly? You could have killed Reilly here with that elevator.'

'Perhaps the clutch slipped,' the man above answered sullenly.

'Perhaps you should get yer frigging finger out of yer frigging arsehole and do yer job properly.'

The worker came down, clumping across the deck in his flapping gumboots. 'I'd like you to take that back, Mr Ross,' he said dourly, brawny arms folded across his chest.

'Go and take a running jump at yersen,' Ross roared. He grabbed the front of the workman's overalls and dragged him towards him. 'Now get back to yer job or I'll frigging well suspend you without pay.'

'You and whose frigging army?' the other man sneered.

Red Ross's temper got the better of him. His right fist slammed out. It caught the workman just under the chin. His head jerked back. Next moment he was falling to the littered deck of the *Margaret Thatcher*, unconscious before he hit it.

Red Ross looked at the others, with their shocked faces. 'Don't look as if you've just got yer frigging monthlies!' he roared. 'Get back to work. Or I'll suspend the frigging lot of you.' Without a second glance to check whether his order was being obeyed – he knew it would – he turned and stalked away. As far as he was concerned the matter was settled.

But for once the big Yorkshireman was wrong. Fifteen minutes later Jacko Simpson came into his little office, handkerchief, stained with his blood, held to his nose. 'Red,' he said thickly.

'What is it?' Ross looked up from his paperwork.

'They forced their way into the radio shack and made me call Hull although it's against company rules. I told them–'

'What did they frigging well want to call Hull for?' Ross interrupted him savagely.

'To tell some bloke there that they were gonna take industrial action.' Jacko stopped and patted his bloody nose once more. 'I'm sorry, Red.'

Red Ross clenched his massive fists angrily. 'It's that sod Jack Hicks,' he snorted. 'He's been trying to get the rigs unionized for years, although the blokes working the rigs get twice the pay his average member does.'

'I don't know about that, Red,' the other man sniffed.

'Yer, get the rigs organized and he'll be in the big time. He'll be off to London as a Labour MP next.' He shook his head angrily. 'Anyhow, what came of the call.'

Jacko Simpson looked at his boots and the gobs of blood on them uneasily.

'Well, come on, spit it out, mate,' Red urged.

'Not very good, Red,' the radio operator said warily; he knew just how explosive the big manager's temper was. 'He told 'em to down tools right off till he saw they got their ... er ... rights.'

Red Ross flushed a brighter red. He slammed his fist against the nearest stanchion, crying, 'Rights ... always fucking rights!'

Chapter Two

Major Honor put down the phone as she knocked on the door of his flat and then entered after he had called, 'Come.' Hilary Stevens, his secretary, looked as beautiful as ever but worried. She put down the sheaf of papers she had brought him to sign before he left for the north and said, 'I wish you weren't going, sir. You know how dangerous those rigs are. There's always accidents happening on them all the time.' For a moment there was a hint of tears in her eyes and he thought she might cry.

'Come on,' he said and touched her hand. 'There's no need to get worried about me.'

She clutched his hand almost hysterically, his big palm firmly gripped in her hot little one. 'The weather's horrible out there and we've heard the daily chopper has been delayed because of it. Why can't someone else go?' She looked up at him pleadingly.

He smiled down at her, touched. 'Because there is no one else and now I've just heard from Red Ross that the men are threatening to down tools. It's something to do with the unions.' He shrugged. 'I've got to be Muggins, I'm afraid.'

She licked her lips, showing those beautiful teeth of hers. 'Can't you wait till the weather improves then?' she suggested. 'If the chopper's not flying, you won't be able to get out anyhow.' She hesitated. 'I'll do anything you want,' she said lamely. 'Anything to make you happy, as long as you'll stay here for a bit longer.'

He was touched and thrilled as well. For the first time for months he felt that old familiar stirring in his loins which he had thought was dead for ever. 'Do you mean that really?'

She lowered her gaze and said huskily, 'Yes, I do. You know I've been in love with you since the first day I came to work for you.' She flushed. 'I've been with other men of course ... but ... but, there can be nobody else like you.' She reached up, standing on the tips of her toes and kissed him suddenly.

He was caught completely off guard. Abruptly she was in his arms and he was kissing her back passionately, as if he were a twenty-year-old himself. Five minutes later he found himself in bed, totally naked, as she was, too.

She saw him off at King's Cross, weeping visibly in the falling snow, as he stowed his case away in the Pullman. Other passengers looked at her curiously. Why was such a pretty girl crying for a distinguished-looking man who could have been her grandfather. Mutely, shoulders heaving, she handed him *The Times*. He caught the headline, 'Germans Put Renewed Pressure on Britain', and thought of von Klarsfeld. He dropped it on his seat and bent down to where she stood on the platform. He kissed her once more. 'Now cheer up, darling,' he urged. 'Everything will be all right. It always is in the end, you know. Problems are there to be solved.'

'I'll never see you again,' she sobbed, shoulders heaving even more, as the guard indicated he should close the door. They were about to leave. Obediently he closed the door, catching only her last tearful words, *'I'll never see you again, Justin.'* Then the train was sliding out of King's Cross heading north. Sadly she turned and made her way out into the snow storm.

Jack Hicks, small, sharp and decisive, finished writing his speech with a flourish. 'That bitch Thatcher thought she had broken us back in the Eighties. Well, brothers, she hadn't. But we must regain our old power. What better symbol to show that lot up in London that we are a force to be reckoned with than to strike the *Margaret Thatcher.* Brothers that will be a message that will go round the whole world.' He mouthed the words triumphantly, as he wrote them. 'Thank you, brothers.' In brackets after that final 'brothers', he added, 'standing ovation'. He stared at the neat handwriting, feeling very proud of himself. It was the kind of rousing speech that the rank-and-file members of the conference would welcome with opening arms. They were sick of all that economic claptrap that the toffee-nosed Londoners were always mouthing these days. He knew his northerners. They wanted basic stuff and he would give them it.

'Jack,' the voice broke into his thoughts.

It was his right-hand man, Jack Jones, his head poked round the open door of his office.

'What's up, Jack?' he asked, seeing from the look on the ex-deckhand's face that there was trouble somewhere.

'There's trouble on the *M.T.*' He pulled the usual contemptuous face they all did when the name of the arch-enemy was mentioned.

'What kind of trouble?'

'They've cut us off. We can't reach the rig over the radio telephone, Jack.'

'They can't do that,' the union boss snapped. 'It's against the law.'

'Well, they have and afterwards if anything comes up they can allus say it had something to do with the weather.' He indicated the window with the snowflakes pelting against it in full white fury.

'Yer, of course, that's just what he would

do. He's right brass necked.'

'You mean that sod, Ross?'

The union boss nodded, his dreams of being a new Arthur Scargill fading a little, at the thought of his opponent. 'I've had a few run ins with the bugger. He's not only a big tough guy. He's cunning as well. He comes from around here, Hornsea way, I think. He knows the men he's dealing with. Give 'em plenty of ale, nooky and money to buy both, and he's got 'em eating out of his hand.' He frowned, and waved his hand in dismissal.

His second-in-command went back into the outer room, telling himself the sooner that Jack Hicks got elected to Parliament, the better. He was an arrogant sort of bastard.

Hicks stared at the flying snow. He knew that if he was going to unionize the *Margaret Thatcher*, which would mean all the new rigs would eventually follow suit, he'd have to do it before the rig struck oil. Those rig men could never see much further than their pay packet and their special bonuses. As soon as the first fat bonus came in, they'd be as happy as pigs in shit.

Somehow he'd have to get one of his people aboard the rig, who would stir things up and get the men on strike before that eventuality. But how? At the moment, the *Margaret Thatcher* was seemingly cut off from the rest of the world and that bastard Red Ross could do exactly as he liked.

Chapter Three

The Palestinian spotted them immediately. They were two big men with short hair and wearing comfortable black shoes. They moved in an easy-going manner as all big men do, shaking the snow off their hats, making a production of it. But their eyes were wary, darting everywhere in the waterfront café-bar, filled with men from the docks, smoking Belga and drinking Jupiter beer. There were even a few eating this lunch hour, hard-boiled eggs and *tartine beurrée*. But mostly they were drinking and discussing in their guttural Flemish Sunday's football match in Brussels. Yes, the Palestinian told himself, as he sipped his café-filtre at the bar, they were cops all right.

He considered what they might know, if anything. They'd be in the Belgian Sûreté all right, so they'd get info from Interpol. That organization had pictures of him, he knew, though they'd be ones that had been taken ten years before when he was very active. But how had they made the connection from Luxembourg to Brussels and got here at Zeebrugge so quickly? That was the mystery.

The girl in Brussels knew only a little part of the scenario, so even if she had talked she could only tell them his first destination. So where had the rest of their info come from? He took another careful sip of the scalding hot coffee and forced a smile at the woman behind the bar in her low cut blouse showing off her wrinkled tits for the sake of the lunchtime crowd of clerks and container handlers.

Was someone else – another organization – betraying him? Had someone known he was crossing Europe for England right from the start? Mossad had no clout these days. Could it have been one of Saddam's own people? He was having trouble with some of his generals, he knew that. He thought of the Yemenis who had sold that German prick, who had once worked for Carlos, to

the *Bundesnachrichtendienst.* * Was it something like that. These days the Germans
could buy virtually everything and anybody,
and they knew it.

Once he had liked them because of what
they had done to the Jews and the way their
Rote Armeefraktion and the Baader-
Meinhoff group had helped the 'cause',
while paying lip-service to the Israelis. But
not now. They were simply concerned with
their own interests and their determination
to be the number one power in Europe. 'It
is the German century again,' he had heard
one of them proclaim proudly at a diplo-
mats' party in Aden, when the German had
been drunk; and he supposed now, as
outside the snowstorm raged, that the
German had been right. It was. Now the
Germans would do anything which served
their own interests, with no regard to those
of others nations. It could be the Germans.

He stopped thinking. The taller of the two
Sûreté men was beginning to move between
the drinkers, asking questions, pausing now

* German Secret Service

97

and again to look at identification cards. Now he knew they were on to something definite. They hadn't come into this café-bar by chance.

He guessed immediately that his *'carte d'identite'* from Meyerode which the dead IRA man had obtained from him, would be compromised. He had to do a bunk.

He put down his cup. *'Die Pissecke bitte?'* he demanded of the blonde with the tired tits behind the bar, sticking to his cover as a German-speaking Belgian. He knew Walloon French (which the French themselves couldn't understand) wouldn't go down well in this Flemish-speaking area.

She pointed to the blanket-covered door, which surprisingly enough had the legend *'La Cour'*, the yard, above it. *'Da langs,'* she said in accented German. These days everyone in Belgium spoke German. It was the language of the future, whatever people in London and Paris said to the contrary.

Slowly, not seeming to be too eager, he moved to the door of the lavatory, body tense, heart beating rapidly, expecting a challenge at any moment. There was none.

He went inside and unzipped his flies, just in case anyone came in. There were the usual obscene drawings, telephone numbers of prostitutes and a machine (in English) advertising condoms ('with bumps that will make the little lady's eyes pop with pleasure'.) He wrinkled his face. What an obscene, degenerate people these Western Europeans were, with their supposed two thousand years of culture.

He made himself forget the obscenities and concentrated on the task at hand. In a minute or two he knew that one of the cops would come out into the back to check if there was anyone there. It was standard operating procedure with cops. He tried the window above the urinal. It was jammed tight. It looked as if it had never been opened for years.

He looked out of the door into the yard itself. The snow was coming down fast, and deadening the noise. Still he could hear the chatter of a police radio from the other side of the wall. There was a police car stationed there, just waiting for someone like him to try to escape over the wall. Again it was normal procedure. He knew then that there was only one way out for him – through the café-bar's entrance. He'd have to fight this one out. But he had the advantage of surprise on his side and there was one thing about cops, he knew that from past experience, they always thought they were the ones who were taking first initiative.

Now he heard the footsteps coming down the stonefloored corridor. This would be the cop, he told himself, coming to do his routine check. The Palestinian tensed. This was it. Hastily he took the steel comb out of his top pocket and prepared for what was to come.

When the big cop came through the door, he was poised in front of the mirror, coming his long black hair carefully with the steel comb. The big cop looked at his dark face in the mirror and the Palestinian could read his mind. He was checking the face with his mental picture of the wanted man. Suddenly the policeman held out a big paw and grunted, 'kaart.'

The Palestinian gave him a careful smile. Comb still in hand, he reached into his pocket as if seeking his identity card and moved towards the waiting policeman. Suddenly, startlingly, he acted. He swept the sharp teeth of the steel comb right across the policeman's broad face underneath the eyes. The skin ripped. Blood started to stream down his face. Caught completely by surprise, the cop staggered back, clutching his bleeding face.

The Palestinian didn't give him a chance to recover. Before he could shout the alarm, the Palestinian grabbed his testicles and twisted hard. The cop went down on his knees, mouth gaping open, as he started to vomit with the intense agony of it all. The Palestinian kicked him hard in the ribs. One of them broke. It stabbed into his lungs like a needle. He fell to the floor on all fours like a boxer refusing to go down for the count. The world revolved in a blood red mist in front of his eyes.

The Palestinian kicked him in the face. He sprawled full length on the wet floor, dead or unconscious, the Palestinian didn't care. All he knew was that the coast was clear for a while.

He sauntered into the bar. In the mirror behind the wet, zinc-covered counter, he could see the other cop with his back to him, checking papers at the far end of the room. He drained the rest of his coffee, dropped a hundred franc note on the counter, smiled at the barmaid with the tired tits, said, 'Keep the change', and went out into the snowstorm. Moments later he was running for the docks.

The docks stretched quite a way from the sea to what had once been Zeebrugge's old fishing port. Most of the trade was with container ships, but the Palestinian knew that two ferry companies ran their ships back and forth to England from the Belgian port, P & O and North Sea Ferries.

Now standing in the falling snow, panting a little, he stood in the shelter of a pile of wooden crates and stared at the section of the dock allotted to North Sea Ferries. Security was lax, he could see that straight away. The company's passenger terminal was wide open with no security fence around it and people entered it without any check. So where did the company's officials do their checking of their passengers? He looked at the big blue and white roll-on, roll-off ferry thoughtfully. It had to be on the ship, he concluded.

He left the shelter of the crates and fought his way through the snowstorm to get a closer look. The foot passengers boarded the ferry by means of a gangway which ran from the top floor of the passenger terminal to the main deck of the ship. There, at the entrance, their boarding cards would be checked and he didn't have one, so that way was out.

He picked up a bucket that someone had left lying about and moved forward purposefully carrying it, as if he were performing some job or other.

The bow ramp of the ferry was up and he could see into the yellow lighted interior, into which the trucks, containers and private cars would go, once they started loading in the afternoon for the evening sailing.

At the moment it was nearly empty save for a couple of containers, but there were no crew members or dockers about. He guessed it was because the dockers and the rest were still having their midday break. This would be as good a time as any to get aboard secretly. He put the bucket down and was about to step onto the ramp, when an officer in a white cap and yellow jacket stepped out of the gloom, checkboard in his hand. Immediately he picked up his bucket and continued with his supposed task. Obviously he would have to find some other way of getting aboard.

Half an hour later he knew how he would do it. The dockers and the fork-lift truck drivers had returned from their break, muffled up to the eyes against the raging snowstorm, which had reduced visibility down to a matter of metres. Expertly drivers hauled the containers into the belly of the ship, changing from one seat to the other as they sped in and out swiftly. Now all was controlled chaos and speed, with the loading master ensuring that the cargo was correctly balanced. They had learned a lot of valuable lessons about such things, since the *Spirit of Free Enterprise* had gone down in this same harbour a few years before.

The Palestinian lay underneath the big Luxglas container. He heard the driver drop into the ankle-deep snow, attach the electric lead to the container and then start up. They started to move. The Palestinian strained every muscle to hang on. The container hit the ramp with a bang that nearly threw him from his precarious perch. He just managed to keep his hold. He felt the sudden warmth of the inside after the piercing cold of the dock. Everywhere there was loud echoing noise, the shriek of brakes, orders, the cloying stench of diesel.

The driver braked. Again he came down from his perch, detached the lead and drove off. The Palestinian waited in the yellow gloom. It was good that he did so. Suddenly he spotted a pair of big boots at the front of the container. There was the rattle of chains. A crewman was securing the container to the deck. Obviously they expected rough seas. A minute later he was finished and the Palestinian was all alone among the containers.

Warily he waited another five minutes, as more and more traffic piled up behind him in the hold. Then when he was sure he was not observed, he crawled out and bent on all fours and peered to all sides. But no one had noticed him. He gave a sigh of relief. Then he grinned. He had done it. He was on his way now.

Chapter Four

Seal reported to the 'Brig' in a seedy pub just off Hull's Hedon Road. He detailed what they had learned so far, while the 'Brig', as lean and as fit as he had been in the Gulf five years before, listened attentively, hardly touching his gin and tonic.

At the pool table in the middle of the room a fat youth with ear-rings, tattoos right up his naked chubby arms, was saying to another youth, 'Don't think you can put one over me, Rod, or I'll shove the fucking cue up your fucking arse.'

Sitting next to the table a frizzy blonde in a micro-mini, drinking a pint of beer, agreed, with, 'That's fucking telling 'im, Rick.' She looked around cockily, as if challenging any of the other patrons to take offence at her language. No one did.

'So we know this, sir,' Seal reported in a low voice. 'This terrorist guy is definitely on

107

his way to the UK. Why else should the illegal's skipper be bringing semtex in. He was to have deposited it in the shallows just off Spurn Point. Special Branch are still grilling him but I think we've already got the most he knows.'

The 'Brig', his hawklike face thoughtful, said, 'So this is the scenario. The terrorist known as the Palestinian is on his way here to carry out some act of sabotage – on account of the semtex – probably at the behest of Saddam Hussein, an act of revenge possibly for his defeat in the Gulf. He can't hit America, so he hits the UK.'

Seal nodded. Behind them at the pool table, the fat lout called Rick was boasting, 'When I've had 'em, mate, they stay mine.' He stuck a finger like a hairy sausage at his chest. 'With a dong like mine, no judy would want to give me up.'

On the chair the frizzy blonde laughed so much that she had to jump to her feet, crying 'I'm off to the loo. I'm pissing mesen!'

'They say Hussein is already developing missiles to reach us, but that'll take some time. So he wants to draw attention to the

108

fact that he can already strike back at his enemies. He's having trouble at home, so he wants some great foreign coup to restore his prestige. The question is – *what?*'

They fell silent, each one of them brooding over their untouched drinks. Fat Rick was boasting, 'Once we had this hoor, about six of us. Up near Cottingham. We clubbed together to have her. And she said, "Lads let yer pants down and let mother see what she's ginna get before I spread 'em" and when she saw mine, she said, "you other lads better go home to yer muvvers. I'm not gonna feel anything *after* that."' He laughed coarsely and the blonde joined in drunkenly, as if it was all a great joke.

The Brig's lean jaw tightened dangerously, but he made no comment. But Seal knew the danger signs. He had seen them before when they had been operating behind Saddam Hussein's lines, the SAS and SBS.

Night after night, as they huddled in their sleeping bags in the freezing desert cold, staring upwards at the infinite velvet and silver sky, he had lectured. 'We have been deprived of our birthright, born into a fourth-rate country which less than half a century ago ruled a third of the world. Then we were confident and knew what we were doing. Now,' he would snort in disgust, 'the gentlemen in Parliament have given us a country full of fat-bellied yobbos, drunks and drug addicts, gimmes living off handouts – all with no pride in themselves or their country.'

'But it has to change,' he had always continued. 'It will change and it can change. Not that fascist nonsense of the Seventies. You know poor David going gaga? It must be done with discipline and not with that so-called parliamentary democracy, with every damned politician snout down in the trough. Whatever their original beliefs, they all end up lord this or that – and rich. Basic principles long forgotten.'

At first Seal had thought him another bullshitter. There were plenty of them about these days in England, ready to bring back the lash and rope. But slowly he had begun to realise the Brig was different. After the Gulf War, he had started getting his 'people', as he called them, in positions of power and influence. But as he always maintained, 'In the end effect, it's the Army which is going to have the say if it comes down to crunches. The Army's still got a sense of discipline and duty. Our first objective is to get our people in power in the Army, always remember that.'

Now as they sat in the working class pub, with its usual bunch of drunken yobbos and cheap bimbos that one saw in pubs throughout the country, Seal realized that the capture of this terrorist, the Palestinian, would be a tremendous publicity coup for the armed services. It would show the general public once again, just as it had done in the Falklands and the Gulf, that of all British institutions, the military knew what they were about; that the soldiers could bring things to a satisfactory con-clusion unlike the bloody politicians in Westminster.

'A rig.' The older man broke their silence suddenly. 'That's it, a rig.' He looked at Seal, face full of new determination.

'What do you mean, sir?' Seal asked a little puzzled.

'Well, ever since that damned business with the Brent Spar rig this summer, rigs have been in the news, now more especially, as the country is developing the new fields to keep us supplied with oil and natural gas way into the next century. If this Palestinian of yours wanted to get into the news, what better way than to hijack a rig?'

Seal whistled softly. 'I see what you mean, sir. But that would be a pretty tall order, for just one man. After all there are fairly large crews on those rigs.'

'I take your point.' The Brig looked hard at him. 'But he won't be alone, will he? As we well know, there are plenty of crackpots and subversives in this country who would help him.'

At the pool table, the fat slob, waiting for the other man to play his shots, had idly taken his cue and was running it up the bimbo's miniskirt, while she shrieked with drunken laughter and wriggled excitedly, as if she couldn't wait to get the real thing. 'Come on, dickhead,' he encouraged the other one, 'let's get it over with. The cow can't wait ter get her gear off, yer can see that.'

The Brig frowned but said nothing. All the same Seal could see that the yobbo's behaviour was upsetting the Brig and when the Brig grew upset things happened, usually very unpleasant things for the person involved.

'So we are perhaps talking about Muslim fundamentalists and the like, the same people who supported Saddam Hussein during the Gulf War, sir?'

'Perhaps, but we could also be talking about our own weirdos, we've got enough of the home grown variety as you well know.'

'Where do we start, sir?' Seal said promptly.

'You stand by with the Alpha Team. I'll get some of our people working on it.'

Seal nodded. He knew the Brig had his 'people', not only in the SAS and other branches of the armed forces, but also in the Special Branch and MI5. He'd find them all right.

'I'll keep in touch. If it is a rig and we can locate it, you'll be in charge of taking them out, my boy.'

'I under–'

Seal didn't finish the sentence for in that instant, the fat yobbo Rick blundered into their table making the glasses shiver and tremble. 'What the fuck!' he exclaimed drunkenly and then seeing the look of absolute contempt on the Brig's face snarled, 'Don't look at me like that, you wrinkled old fart. When you grow up, you might become a garden dwarf.' He laughed uproariously at his own wit and the blonde shrieked with him. But not for long.

With surprising speed for a man in his fifties, the Brig moved. His middle finger shot out. With full force, he drove it into the yobbo's balls. The latter shrieked with pain and doubled up, mouth open and gaping for breath. As he doubled up and his head came down, the Brig brought up his clenched fist. It caught the other man squarely on the chin. He gave another gasp and flew backwards to smash against the wall, along which he slithered slowly and foolishly till he was slumped on the dirty floor, vomit trickling from his slack mouth.

The Brig rose. 'Come on my boy, let's get out of this dump.'

Seal finished off his drink and rose, too, to follow the Brig to the door. As he passed the bar, the Brig said to the sloven man, with a pearl clip in his ear, who stood behind it, 'Better sweep away that rubbish ... before it starts to stink.' Then they were outside in the snow.

Chapter Five

Less than a mile away, Major Honor emerged from Hull's Paragon Street Station and looked for the company car. There it was, a Rolls Royce, with the logo of UK Oil, a rig set against a union jack, flying on its bonnet flag. The grey-uniformed chauffeur spotted him immediately. He signalled with his headlights and began to drive slowly through the snow towards the waiting oilman.

As he waited a scruffy beggar with a shaggy dog sidled up to Honor. On his chest he bore a crude notice stating, that he was 'hungry and homeless'. Honor told himself that the beggar's intricate haircut must have cost at least twenty pounds. 'Can you spare some change, guy?' the man whined, while the dog slumped on its hind legs, as if were weary of life.

'No I can't,' Honor snapped. He knew

there was a whole class of young men these days who lived from begging and 'the social', as they called their free meal ticket, the Department of Social Security. They had never worked and never would, if they could help it.

The beggar looked at him, was about to swear, then changed his mind. He slouched off, followed by the dog to the shadows from which they had come.

The chauffeur opened the door and got out. He opened the other one for Honor. 'Had a nice trip up, sir?' he asked.

'Yes, thanks Charles.' Honor frowned as the snow kept tumbling down as if it would never stop again. 'What does met say at the helipad?'

'Not too bright, sir,' the chauffeur said, as they got into the Rolls, 'much of the same. But the Jolly Green Giant says he'll have a go. You know him, sir.'

'I certainly do.' Honor chuckled at the memory of the helicopter pilot, Ed Halberstadt, a big fat fellow who had fought in Vietnam and bore a silver plate in the back of his shaven head as a souvenir of that war.

The Jolly Green Giant would take any kind of a risk to get supplies and mail to 'my joes', as he called the rig workers, 'The Pony Express must get through.' 'If anyone can do it, it'll be the Jolly Green Giant,' Honor remarked.

The chauffeur waited as a taxi discharged its passenger, a tall erect man in tweeds. Soldier, or ex-soldier, Honor told himself automatically as the Brig strode away to catch his train. Then they were moving into the traffic...

The snow storm buffetted the *Margaret Thatcher* with its full fury now. Sometimes the wind howled around the rig with a strange kind of eerie keening; sometimes it struck the rig with angry punches, like blows from a gigantic fist. Mostly however, it smashed the rig with a furious shriek, throwing up the heaving grey-green water in solid walls, as if it wanted to thrust this man-made abomination down to the depths.

Down in the mess the oilmen's conversation almost ceased. The TV went and

Radio Humberside was distorted by constant static. So they sat there in that crazy heaving wild world, barely sipping their cans of McEwan's Ale, eyes fearful, as if they knew the storm was about to devour them.

Two cooks came staggering in with piles of sandwiches in greaseproof paper, clothes covered with snow. 'Bully beef butties, lads. All we can do,' they shouted above the roar of the wind. 'Stoves have gone out.'

One of the fearful disgruntled men picked up a packet and threw it at the bulkhead. 'That's no frigging grub to give a bloke who's been grafting all day. We want hot grub.'

Red Ross, his normally crimson face white with snow, appeared in the doorway. He sneered, 'Grafting yer sez. You've been sitting on yer fat arse all day more like it. Now shift yersens. The Jolly Green Giant's coming in soon and we need the landing lights on. Move it!'

The news cheered them up. There'd be the *Sun* and the Page Three Girls and the *Hull Daily Mail*, even letters. They 'moved it', one of them saying as he passed Red Ross,

'I asked our lass to send us some porn for the video. I hope she hasn't forgotten.' Red Ross shook his head in mock disbelief and then he followed them to the helipad, where already the first of them were switching on the lights and straining their eyes for the first glimpse of the chopper.

Then there he was, his broad American voice booming over the amplifier, 'OK down there, I'm coming and I've a VIP with me, so no frigging slip-ups.'

Suddenly into the white burst of glistening light, the chopper burst into view, hovering desperately above the swaying platform below. Red Ross clenched his fists. This was going to be hairy, he told himself.

Suddenly Red Ross knew he shouldn't let the big fat American do it, for he suspected the VIP was the Major. He didn't want him killed as well. He picked up his own mike and turned up the amplifier. 'Don't do it. Give it another hour or so. The storm might have peaked by then.'

'Easy as pissing in a pot,' the American boomed cheerfully. 'Nothing like the stuff we did in Nam. Over and out.' His amplifier went dead suddenly.

Red Ross cursed. He knew the Yank. When he decided to do something, he'd do it. He was a stubborn old bastard.

Now the roar of the chopper was ear-splitting. The plane seemed to dance in the air, as the American tried to co-ordinate his descent with the momentary tilt of the platform. Red Ross bit his bottom lip. All around him the crew were silent, ignoring the storm, totally, completely fascinated by the attempt to get the plane down in one piece.

By now the Jolly Green Giant was hovering less than twenty yards up.

Time and time again the chopper was buffeted by the storm and an anxious Red Ross could hear how the pilot gunned the engine in a frantic attempt to avoid being blown away. Suddenly the amplifier clicked on again and the Jolly Green Giant's voice boomed hollowly, 'The s.o.b looks like a Coney Island roller coaster, but here we *go!*'

The sound died away and then the chopper was falling. Red Ross dug his nails into the palms of his hands till it hurt. The noise was overpowering. The roar of the storm, the clatter of the chopper's rotors, the clatter of the empty coke cans on the platform, dancing and skipping around in the prop wash.

Like a giant black metallic hawk the chopper fell out of the sky. Red Ross prayed. To no avail. The rotor struck the derrick on the port side of the rig. The chopper lurched violently, but still kept flying. *'Duck'* Red Ross yelled frantically as the severed blade hissed lethally through the air. The next rotor went. *'Oh my sodding shitting Christ!'* a crewman yelled as the next rotor went and then the chopper was falling over the side, engine shrieking as the American gave her full power – but again to no avail.

Red Ross craned his neck, face horrified and shocked, as he watched the crippled helicopter plummet into the sea. Then he sprang into action. 'Come on, lads. Let's help 'em!'

Honor grabbed hold of the American's jacket and yelled above the roar of the waves surging all around them. 'Come on, we'll go under in a minute.' He shook the pilot violently, almost angrily. There was no response save that the pilot's head lolled to one side. Then in the green gloom, with the lights flickering and threatening to go out at any moment, a horrified Honor saw why. The joystick had pierced the pilot's chest just where the heart was. The Jolly Green Giant was dead.

For a moment Major Honor was paralysed, unable to move. Then he heard the sheering, rending noise of metal being torn away. The helicopter was breaking up under the pounding of the waves. He had to get out while there was still time. He took one last look at the dead pilot and then he grabbed for the door. He heaved it. It didn't move. Now the waves were parallel with the shattered cockpit. Red-faced with the effort, he tugged at the door again, exerting all his strength. It gave. He breathed sigh of relief. Then the icy cold water was striking his body angrily and he was gasping for breath, as he tried to grab for the nearest stanchion. But it seemed as if the sea was determined to have him. The waves beat at him furiously and submerged him. He came up, spluttering for breath, body rapidly turning to ice.

He knew from the reports he had read on the subject that he had only seconds to live if he didn't get out of the freezing water soon. Summoning up his last reserves of strength, he waited till the waves sank to the trough, then he struck out. His right hand caught something wet and slippery. It was a stanchion. He thanked God and tugging his other arm out of the boiling, angry water caught the stanchion with that hand, too.

For a moment he just hung there, unable to do any more. The waves submerged. He choked and spluttered, shaking his head, trying not to let himself be sucked down by them. He reached up his right hand. It found another stanchion. The barnacles cut into his palms. He didn't notice the pain. He was escaping the sea – that was all he was concerned with. Painfully slowly, he seized the higher stanchion with his other hand, feeling the strength ebb from him. At his feet the waves hissed and growled like some evil predator determined not to be deprived of its prey.

Gasping for breath, vision blurred, a dull

roaring in his ears now, he sought and found yet another higher piece of metal. But his strength was ebbing away rapidly and he was gasping as if he were running a great race; and still the waves roared at his feet, trying to tug him down into its green greedy maw.

Suddenly a strong hand gripped his right one. 'Hang on in there, Major,' a voice called from a long long way off. He gasped with relief and then he was being drawn upwards. A moment later he blacked out...

He coughed and spluttered as the strong whisky ran down his throat. He opened his eyes and everything swung into focus. Red Ross was bending over him, a worried look on his tough face. In the centre of the room, his sodden clothes had been spread out, while over a chair there hung a shirt, a sweater and a boiler suit with the UK Oil logo on its back. He himself was muffled in a thick blanket.

Red Ross wiped the back of his hand across his forehead, 'Thank God, you've come to, Major. For a while we didn't think you'd make it. That sea was freezing.'

He forced himself to smile and said, 'You're telling me.' Then his smile vanished. 'The Jolly Green Giant's dead,' he added.

Ross nodded. 'We thought so. Poor sod.'

Honor told himself that that was as good an epitaph as any. They were all poor sods on the *Margaret Thatcher*. The rig seemed to have a jinx on her. All who came into contact with the rig seemed to get into trouble. He took another sip of the strong single malt and asked a little shakily, 'What's the situation, Red?'

'Improved a bit. I think the Jolly Green Giant croaking like that had an effect. There's been no more talk of downing tools – at least for the time being.' He scratched his unshaven chin. 'You know, Major, all of us connected with this industry are a pretty unusual bunch. I mean, what other blokes would work them crippling twelve hour shifts under such shitty conditions, even for the extra pay? Then eight hours' kip, a shit, shave and a shampoo and then back at it on the kind of lousy grub them so-called cooks of ours dish up. And that for fourteen solid days with no betting shops, pubs and no hot nookie at night from wifey when you go home from work.'

'I suppose it's the challenge, Red,' Honor said thoughtfully and feeling new energy surging through his blood with the fire of the whisky. 'A bunch of chaps fighting the elements and nature like in a war, all working towards a common aim, knowing that if one lets the team down the whole thing could collapse.'

Red nodded his understanding. 'Something like that, I suppose, Major. In my way of thinking they're not a bad lot. You've just got to lead them right.'

'We will, Red,' Honor assured the big foreman. He rose and let the blanket drop. Red Ross could see the gnarled scars on his side and right shoulder where he had been struck by shrapnel from a Chinese mortar bomb so long before. 'Pass me those duds, please. It's about time we all got back to work.'

Red Ross handed him the thermal underwear. Honor pulled on the pants and said, iron in his voice, now, 'Red we'll get that oil up before this week's out, even if we've got to dig it up with our bloody naked hands...'

At the outside of the door, the crewman who Red had floored earlier that long day, whispered to himself contemptuously, 'Silly bastards. They've got another think coming.' Then he slipped away noiselessly in his ragged trainers like a rat slinking into the safety of its hole.

Day Three

Wednesday

'My experience is that the gentlemen who are the best behaved and the most sleek are those who are doing the mischief. We cannot be too sure of anybody.'

Field Marshal Lord Ironside,
Chief of the Imperial General Staff,
Summer 1940

Chapter One

'Guten Morgen, meine Damen und Herren. Es ist sechs Uhr dreissig. Das Fruhstuck wired jetzt in der Cafeteria serviert.' The rather posh German recorded announcement was followed by the Dutch, *'U wordt vriendelijk'*, then in French. Finally the message came in English. 'It is six-thirty, breakfast is now being served in the cafeteria.' Although this was a British ship, it was as if the authorities realized which nationalities were the most important. Britons came obviously at the bottom of the pecking order.

The Palestinian allowed himself a slight smile at the thought, then he followed the crowd from the reclining seat deck into breakfast, wrinkling his nose at the smell of that forbidden meat, bacon.

He avoided a crowd of noisy French kids heading for England on a 'mini cruise', as North Sea Ferries called the three day round trip very grandly, and selected a bowl of cereal. Morosely he hunched over it and stared through the window at the grey water and slick mud banks of the Humber estuary. In an hour they would be docking in Hull. He told himself he would have to be ready by then.

He had spent most of the previous evening in the lounge, crowded with elderly German tourists, dripping with cheap gold jewellery, sombre-looking Dutch businessmen, drunken soldiers and their girlfriends, going home on leave from the British Army of the Rhine. All had been noise, smoke, drunken oaths and the shouts of the croupiers at the various gaming tables.

He had drunk his glass of tonic and had watched them in disgust. He was no longer the idealist he had been twenty years before, but he still felt the same disgust as he had then at the decadence and lack of discipline of Western society. One day Islam would settle with them for good and that would be an end to the corruption and loose-living they had spread throughout the world.

At ten that night he had stolen the

blankets and pillows collected by one of the Germans – you had to show your boarding card to get them – and gone off to the area of reclining seats. There he feigned asleep straight away to avoid having to answer questions from the crew or his fellow passengers.

He had managed to get a good sleep between midnight, when the last of the noisy drunkards had departed, until four. While it was still, the only sound the snores of the others and the steady throb of the ship's engines, as the ferry plodded steadily across the North Sea, he had stolen a razor from the open sponge bag of a fat middle-aged German and had gone to complete his toilet in the below deck shower rooms reserved for the truck drivers on board.

Now showered, shaved and relatively well-rested, he concentrated on the next task: how to get off the ferry without being apprehended. He knew from his own early days in rainy, dreary grey old London as a student at the London School of Economics, just what swines the English immigration authorities could be, especially to those who weren't white.

Superficially polite in their dark suits and green striped ties of the Intelligence Corps, with that compulsory 'sir' at the end of every question, their eyes always remained hard and suspicious. They distrusted anyone who didn't hold their own passport with its ancient coat-of-arms. And security at Hull wouldn't be as lax as at Zeebrugge. He knew that from other comrades.

He pondered the problem, as Immingham slid by, smoke belching from its chimneys, and next to the buffet a group of French school children on a 'cultural visit' started throwing breadrolls at each other. A steward stopped them, after being hit himself by one of the rolls and passed the Palestinian's table, darkly muttering, 'Bloody frogs. We should never have gone into it.' What 'it' was, the Palestinian didn't know. He was not interested either; he was too busy concentrating on his problem.

A soldier in camouflaged uniform slumped down opposite him. He had circles under his eyes and looked pale. 'Christ, what a night,' he said apropos of nothing.

'Me mouth feels like the bottom of parrot's cage.' He took a deep drink of his tea, as if he were very thirsty and looked out of the window in mild disgust. 'Looks as if it's gonna rain agen, mate. Bloody miserable place Hull – don't know why any sod would want to live there. Gimme Leeds any time.' He took another deep drink and licked his parched lips. 'Wonder if they'll open the bar before we dock.'

Politely the Palestinian looked at his wrist-watch. It was exactly seven o'clock. 'Doubt it,' the Palestinian said. 'Won't be long before we get there.'

'Sod it then,' the soldier said. 'No matter, though. Me mates from Catterick are picking me up. They allus have a few buckshee brews in cans in the truck. I'll have to wait till then. But they allus let squaddies through first, that is when they're in uniform. Ta, ta, gonna get mesen some more char.'

Uniform! The idea flashed through his mind immediately: an instant ready-made idea for getting through immigration. He finished his cereal and went. When the soldier came back and sat in the empty seat, he mumbled, 'Didn't know I was doing him a favour, talking to him – and him a bloody wog.'

He had picked a good time for the task on hand. Most of the passengers were either eating or getting ready to eat. The crew, those on duty, were below decks, preparing to unload. As a result the upper decks, still quite dark in the grey rainy dawn, were virtually deserted. The Palestinian walked up the deck towards the bow until he came to a chain suspended from the railing, which bore the sign, *'Private – Crew Only'*.

He looked to left and right. There was no one in sight, save for a fat black cook in white hat and singlet, emptying a carton of trash over the side before they got into Hull, and trying to keep the screaming seagulls, which fluttered all around him greedily, from getting at the waste. Swiftly he skipped over the chain and crouching low he moved forward, bobbing up at regular intervals to peer through the portholes of the officers' cabins.

The first one was no good. A bespectacled

138

officer with his tunic undone was drinking a mug of coffee at his desk and reading what looked like a report. The second porthole was equally no good. The blind was drawn and because the window was steamed, he guessed that someone was still sleeping in there; perhaps the officer had been on night shift work. He moved on.

The third looked more likely. It was empty. There was a half empty bottle of scotch on the little table next to an open magazine opened to show a girl in stockings and black underwear. Most importantly, hanging from the pegs on the door was a white officer's cap with next to it a dark merchant marine tunic.

The Palestinian hesitated no longer. Swiftly, silently, he entered the nearest door and hurrying down the dimly lit corridor paused just outside the door to the third cabin. He tapped lightly just in case the officer was in the combined toilet and shower into which he had not been able to see from outside. There was no response. Hurriedly he opened the door, tugged down the tunic and hat and shoved them inside his jacket. Just in time.

Just as he reached the gangway once more outside, a black steward, with an apron tied around his waist, came towards him carrying a pail of slops. He pointed a finger at the sign stating 'Private – Crew Only'.

The Palestinian flashed him a brilliant smile and muttered something in Arabic before brushing by the black man. 'Bloody foreigner,' the steward muttered and threw the slops at the shrieking seagulls.

Thirty minutes later the ship was emerging slowly from the lock at King George's Dock and heading for its mooring place on the opposite side.

Already the excited group tours and foot passengers were assembling with their baggage in the lounge, while the public address system blared its announcements to those who drove in vehicles in four languages, 'Wir bitten zu Ihren PKW zu begeben ... de vous rendre vers votre vehicle pour ... U wardt vriendelijk verzacht.' As before the announcement in English came last, 'You are kindly requested to return to your vehicle'

But the Palestinian had no time for such

matters now. In the toilet of the lounge, he looked at himself in the mirror. He had torn off the officer's insignia from the cap and put the tunic on under his black raincoat, leaving the latter open.

It was drizzling again outside, so he had a good excuse for the civilian raincoat. He guessed he looked fairly official. He suspected they no longer had porters on these package tour ferries – he had heard no mention of porters being available in the flurry of announcements coming from the public address system. But the passengers wouldn't know that. He made up his mind. He'd have a try.

He went outside and mingled with the throng of passengers, some of them already taking photos of the ferry terminal, as if it was of great architectural beauty. His dark eyes flashed to left and right. Then he spotted what he was looking for. A fat overdressed German woman, sitting on one case and clutching another bag in her hands nervously. She was obviously alone and worried. Perhaps this was her first trip to England.

He went over to her and said softly, 'Can I help you, madam?'

She looked at him a little helplessly and said, '*Wie bitte?*'

He flashed her a smile. '*Kann ich Ihnen helfen?*' he asked in his careful German. He indicated her bags. '*Mit Ihrem Gepack?*'

'*Ach* so,' she said, giving him a gold-toothed smile. '*Sehr liebenswurdig von Ihnen.*'

Hastily he picked up her bags and before she could stop him he was pushing his way forward through the throng which was now heading for passenger ramp that led to the top floor of the terminal. She trotted after him trustingly.

The Palestinian looked down. The long line of cars, their exhausts jetting white-grey in the damp cold, were moving slowly towards the two booths which contained the immigration officials. From there the white lines indicating in which direction to go ran the length of the terminal and went round the corner.

He guessed that meant the customs officials would be there at the entrance. With a bit of luck, therefore, there would be no kind of authorities up at this level. He made his decision just as he reached the top of the gangway and the entrance to the terminal.

'Must have a quick piss,' he said to the security guard who stood there. 'Taken short. Keep an eye on the bags will yer?'

Before the man could respond, he was gone, leaving the bags behind with the security guard suddenly flustered as he tried to prevent the gaggle of old ladies from falling over them. Swiftly the Palestinian darted into the building, eyes reading the signs as he moved. An arrow to the left and the walking figure of a man. The men's toilets. He went down the corridor towards it at speed. There was no one about. He opened the door to the toilets. No one was there save for a pair of hair bare legs with overalls around the ankles in the furthest cubicle. Then his eyes fell on the donkey jacket hanging from the hook. It had North Sea Ferries written across the back in large letters. His heart leapt. Obviously it belonged to the man sitting on the lavatory. It was almost too easy.

In an instant he removed the stolen jacket and tossed away the white cap. He started to slip into the donkey jacket which smelled of male sweat and diesel oil. He wrinkled his nose in disgust. It was then that the water flushed and the door of the cubicle started to open.

The Palestinian knew he could not evade being spotted. So he acted. The burly docker was still zipping up his flies when the Palestinian gave him a karate chop across the throat. The man went out like a light. Not even a grunt of pain. He flew backwards and fell into the toilet foolishly, trousers down about his knees, the water flushing his buttocks.

The Palestinian slammed the door closed after him. It would be a while till he came back to consciousness. Still he couldn't waste a precious second. Every moment spent in the terminal spelled danger.

He went out. Down below, the place was full of foot passengers who had passed through customs and were waiting for their party's coach to take them to wherever they were going, or the buses that would carry them to Hull's railway station. Suddenly he started. There was a uniformed policeman mixing with them and it was clear from the look in his eyes that he was searching for someone.

Had they discovered the missing jacket and cap on board the ferry and put two and two together? He didn't know, but he daren't take a chance.

He backed off and headed for the little second floor cafeteria. He bought a cup of tea from a bored sleepy attendant and picked up a copy of yesterday's *Hull Daily Mail* from the counter where he paid. He pretended to be interested in the headline – '*Two elderly sisters raped and clubbed to death*', it read – as he walked to a chair. In reality, his dark eyes were searching the area below for anything suspicious. Yes, there it was. A white van with the word, 'Police' written on it in blue. He nodded to himself. That confirmed it. The police had been specially summoned here. Why else would they be at the terminal at eight o'clock in the morning?

The Palestinian's mind raced. For a little

while he was safe, he supposed. But if the authorities had sent a van, he concluded there had to be more than one policeman. Obviously they'd search the whole terminal in due course, including the toilets. Then they'd find the still unconscious docker. Time was running out fast. What the hell was he going to do?

He finished his tea with a gulp. He realized what to do now. The police would be obviously expecting him to attempt to leave the dock. He wouldn't do them that favour. Not just yet at least. Down below he had spotted a group of dockers heading for the wharfside. Obviously they were just going on shift. Well, he'd do the same. Minutes later, carrying a shovel – ripped from the wall next to the firebucket with its sand – he was marching rapidly after the others, whistling merrily as if he hadn't a care in the world. The policeman standing next to the van talking into his radio didn't even give him a second glance.

Chapter Two

'Good afternoon, Brigadier, how are you?'

The Brig turned startled. He hadn't anticipated anyone recognizing him on a crowded Shaftesbury Avenue at one o'clock on Wednesday afternoon.

It was Leo Cooper, the military publisher, smiling in his usual urbane manner, together with his secretary, whom the Brig vaguely remembered was called Georgina. 'Hello Leo,' he said. 'How are you?' he asked without interest, his eyes scanning the crowd, looking for his contact.

'Business is busy as always, but otherwise all right, Brigadier. We're just off to the Oporto – the pub,' Cooper added hastily. 'Our HQ as we call it. Fancy a drink? I'd like to talk to you about your book. I'm sure you've got a lot of fascinating stuff to relate – and you know just how well SAS books sell.'

The Brig chuckled, mind on other things. 'Long past, it, Leo. Gone a bit dotty, you know. With age.'

Now it was time for the publisher to chuckle. 'Oh, pull the other one, Brigadier. You and dotty. I bet you you're up to your eyes in things at this very minute.'

The Brig shot the publisher a hard look, but Cooper didn't seem to notice it. He said, 'Well, Brigadier, any time you want to talk business, please call me. We can have lunch together at Garrick. Goodbye.'

'Goodbye, Leo,' the Brig said and waited until the publisher and his secretary had turned the corner and vanished in the direction of the Oporto public house. He did so deliberately. He knew little of the publishers' world. But what he did know told him that the people in the book business were inveterate gossips. He didn't want anyone repeating anything about his present contact. He might well put her life at danger.

'Hello, Brigadier,' a voice said behind him. He turned swiftly. It was her. 'Hello, Daisy, good to see you again.' He looked at the woman. She was paler than usual and there were dark circles under her eyes, but her gaze was as direct and as intelligent as ever. 'A drink?' he asked.

She nodded eagerly. 'Love one, Brigadier. Feeling a bit fragile at the moment.'

He looked concerned. 'Can't you shake the damn things, Daisy? They'll kill you in the end.'

'I know,' she answered seriously. 'But without them I couldn't keep going. Not with the kind of life I lead.' She put her arm through his and looked up at him lovingly. 'Now dear Brigadier, lead me to that nice strong drink.'

He patted her hand. Hard man that he was, he was moved.

Daisy Cummings had been the best junior Intelligence officer working for him back in the Eighties in Northern Ireland – and sometimes in Southern Ireland, too. In 1989 she had been snatched by a gang of IRA men who had been running in drugs from the Continent to sell in the UK to pay for arms bought in the States. They had soon beaten the information they had wanted out of her – he had always told his undercover people not to risk their lives by withholding information – then had proceeded to gang-rape her, all eight of them.

Next morning an undercover patrol of the SAS had found her in a ditch near the border, naked and bruised all over. Worse than that, she had been in a state of total shock. In a month or so she had appeared to have recovered, but the Army's own special investigation branch had found drugs in her possession.

She had told them, 'After what happened to me, I can't function without them,' but they had remained unmoved. He had gone in to bat for her personally, but the authorities had been adamant. She had been dismissed from the service. Since then, still on drugs, ruining her body, but with her mind as alert as ever, she had worked for him.

Now, as they sat in the dimly lit bar, as far away from the staff as possible, he asked her, 'Well?'

She took the cigarette out of her mouth, her intelligent eyes wrinkled against the blue

150

smoke curling up about her face. 'As you know, Brigadier, I've been going to bed with Aziz, ever since you suspected he was one of them.'

He nodded gravely, wondering how she could do it, but telling himself that Daisy Cummings would do anything to get the country out of the mess it was in. She'd even sleep with the enemy.

'I got him drunk last night. It wasn't difficult. They have no head for alcohol, but all of them love it despite their creed. Anyway, sir, after he had finished sticking it in me–'

The Brigadier winced at the expression and the vision it conjured up.

'He got pretty pissed and started to talk. Most of it was drunken waffle. They do like to appear to be big men.'

She broke off and stared at the door. A party of Japanese tourists had just come in, all spectacles, cameras and new overlong raincoats bought from Harrods. Immediately the waiters sprang into action, obviously expecting good tips. They were all over the slightly bewildered Japanese, who huddled together as if they were afraid of being split off from the main party, bowing repeatedly, helping them off with their coats, directing them to their seats as if they were royalty.

'Bloody Nips,' a waiter exclaimed out of the side of his mouth 'but at least they spend money.'

Daisy laughed a little harshly and the Brigadier guessed she had already had a fix this morning. 'What a country,' she exclaimed contemptuously. 'What lengths we'll go to make a few bob. Where was I?'

He told her and she continued. 'Well, as I said, most of his stuff was waffle. But it was clear that he is involved in some big op. They've got a guy coming from the Middle East to run it. He's a big time operator. Aziz was very proud to be associated with this guy.'

'Any idea of their target?' the Brigadier asked hopefully, telling himself she was talking about the Palestinian; it had to be him.

'No,' she answered and looked pointedly at her glass which was empty.

The Brigadier signalled to the waiter. He left the Japanese reluctantly. 'They say if we can lay on a belly dancer, they'll put in twenty quid a head into the pot. Wow!'

The Brigadier ignored the waiter's statement. He said sharply like a man long used to giving orders – and having them obeyed, 'A double G and T for the lady please – and don't take all day about it, *please*.'

The waiter shot him a look, but said nothing.

'One thing though,' she said after the waiter had gone. 'Aziz said the comrades,' she sneered at the word, 'up in the north will be looking for him when he arrives. In other words nobody down here in the smoke will be involved.'

'That's useful,' the Brigadier remarked thoughtfully, as the waiter deposited the glass in front of Daisy. The waiter said excitedly, 'We've got one. She's coming right over from Shaftesbury Avenue. She'll do a half hour show for fifty quid. Money for old rope today.'

'Anything else?'

She took a greedy gulp at her drink and said, 'Naturally I tried to pump him where exactly in the North. I mentioned Bradford, but he said that Bradford was out. The Special Branch had got it sewn up – ever since the riots.'

'But has it got to be a place with a large Muslim or fundamentalist population?' he asked as if thinking aloud.

'Search me,' she answered with a careless shrug.

'You know I'd dearly love to, Daisy,' he beamed, gently squeezing her hand.

'Oh no you wouldn't, Brigadier. You wouldn't want to touch me with a barge pole.' Suddenly there were tears in her eyes.

He pressed her hand harder. 'Daisy, don't be silly. You're a good girl.'

Her tears vanished. She laughed cynically. 'That's the best bloody joke of the year.'

Five minutes later the belly dancer appeared and they left.

Chapter Three

They had been working flat out during the morning. Not more than one hundred yards away the North Sea was boiling angrily as the escaping gas erupted on the surface. Both the Major and Red Ross knew it was dangerous to work under these conditions, but as Red Ross had remarked on starting the shift, 'I know it's one hell of a risk. One spark and the whole damned thing could go up in flames. But I'm playing it cool. No smoking. Keep the lighting down to a minimum. Have the electricians check the gear every hour.' He'd laughed and ended with, *'Then frigging well pray!'*

Major Honor didn't know whether the big Yorkshireman had actually prayed, but so far their luck had held. Now and again the escaping gas had belched obscenely vomiting a thick jet of water into the grey sky, with each time Honor holding his breath and wondering if this time the gas would ignite. But nothing had happened and work had continued, the crew cursing all the time, for the galleys had been put out and in spite of the freezing weather there was only cold food and soft drinks on call.

At midday Red Ross turned to a worried Honor and said, as gas jetted upwards in a flurry of wild water yet again, 'All right, Major, this is what I'm proposing. I'm going to keep on operating for a little while longer – as long as them jets don't get no worse. If they do, I'll kill the gas.'

The Major sniffed. 'How will you do it?' he asked a little uncertainly, knowing the risks they were already running.

'I'll pump in gel and kill the flow that way.'

Major Honor looked alarmed. He knew the process from his own days when he had worked in the field on rigs. A slanting hole would be drilled into the side of the leak and the gel, a grey powder, would be pumped in to form a heavy mud. With luck it might close or stop the gas leak. 'But if you do that,' he objected, 'it might mean the end of our drilling for oil.'

'Exactly, Major!' Red Ross looked at his worried face and knew what he was thinking. But he told himself perhaps this time they'd have luck on their side before anything else went wrong. 'Don't worry, sir,' he said encouragingly. 'We'll make it. Come on, Major, let's go and have a cuppa.'

Twenty feet away, Hurst, the crewman whom Red Ross had floored, was eating a stale sandwich in disgust, the tea poured from the last thermos growing cold at his elbow. He eyed his opposite number, big Slack (from big slack arse), a Geordie with an enormous gut and rear, and moaned, 'Bloody awful nosh. How can those sods up top expect a bloke to work a twelve hours shift in the middle of December, with yer balls being frozen off on nosh like this.'

Big Slack took his eyes off the 'crotch art' which was stuck to the walls of the crew's mess deck everywhere and said, 'She's got a nice beaver, that one. Real blow-dried, dyed public hair.' He licked his lips fondly.

'Pubic hair,' Hurst corrected him routinely, runtish face angry at the big Geordie's stupidity. 'I was saying the nosh is 'orrible.'

''Cos they put the galley fires out,' Big Slack said, as if that explained everything.

'I know you silly sod. But why have they put 'em out? I'll tell yer fer free,' he snorted, ''Cos they don't want that escaping gas to go up.'

'I suppose yer right,' Big Slack said, as if he hadn't thought about it before.

'Of course I'm right, and if that sod goes up, we go up with it, get it?'

'Don't piss in yer pants, Hurstie,' the other man answered calmly, turning his attentions to the 'crotch art' once more. 'It ain't happened yet, has it?' He laughed.

'Silly fart. Course it ain't. But when it does, you'll be laughing at t'other side of yer cakehole, *I don't think*.'

Big Slack Arse took his gaze off a nubile blonde with shaven pubes, who was seemingly admiring the splendid thing she had between her legs in a silver mirror. 'Luvverly grub!' he enthused, licking his lips once more greedily.

Angrily Hurst threw down the rest of his stale sandwich onto the littered mess table. 'Ain't you got no sense?' he demanded. 'It only takes some arsehole to sneak off to the heads to have a crafty fag and - *whoosh* - we all go up to outer space.'

For the first time since the conversation had commenced, Slack Arse looked serious. 'Never thought of it like that, Hurstie,' he said solemnly. 'Some of the blokes on this rig don't have no sense.'

Nor do you, you fat Geordie bastard, Hurst told himself. Aloud, he said, 'No, sooner or later it's gonna blow if we don't stop it.'

Slack Arse looked puzzled. 'But what can we do? That's why they give us fat bonuses for the risks we take.'

'What good's a fat bonus if you're sitting on a cloud, playing a frigging harp?' Hurst sneered.

'But we've got the chopper if anything goes wrong,' Big Slack objected.

'Yer, the little one with seats for the pilot and two others, and d'yer know who them two others would be?'

Big Slack shook his head in bewilderment, the 'crotch art' forgotten altogether now, as the risks they were taking started to penetrate his thick shaven skull.

'Well, I'll tell yer, Mister bloody Major Honor and that big git Red Ross. They'd be off and us suckers would be left behind to be grilled nice and crisp.'

Slack Arse shuddered at the mental picture. 'But what can we do?' he asked.

Suddenly Hurst bit his bottom lip, as he realized that soon there would be no going back. If he took the step he intended to, there'd be all hell to pay if he failed.

'Well?' Big Slack demanded, as outside the escaping gas plopped with sinister silent insistency.

Hurst broke his silence, his mind made up. 'Get the rest of the off duty shift in here, even if you have to pull 'em out of their racks and then I'll tell yer what we're going to do to stop them two buggers playing the lottery with our frigging lives...'

Chapter Four

They sat together, Seal and the little grey man from MI5, in the car-park at Hull's Paragon Street station. It was snowing again outside and it suited their purpose as they conferred on the situation. People, heads bent against the whirling snowflakes, weren't interested in hanging about. They just wanted to get out of the snow.

'Well,' the MI5 man said, the end of his nose red with the cold, 'this is what we know so far. One,' he ticked off the statement with one finger of his gloved hand, 'our man's started at Lux Airport. There he left behind him the dead body of his IRA contact.'

Seal nodded his agreement and turned on the engine of his car once more, to bring some heat into the freezing interior.

'Two, the illegals were running in semtex for him to be cached off the mouth of the Humber. We got on to that one, too.'

Seal took out a small silver flask of whisky and offered it wordlessly to the MI5 man. He accepted it and took a hefty gulp before saying, 'Thank you. That's better. Three,' he continued, 'he was spotted in Zeebrugge and on a North Sea Ferry sailing for Hull from there. Since then the trail has gone dead. But Captain Seal, he's here. Now what is he going to do?'

For a moment Seal thought it was a rhetorical question, but then when he saw the look of bewilderment in the other man's eyes, he knew it wasn't. So he said, 'It's a rig, sir. I'm sure he's going to attack a rig. It can't be a ferry – we've already been through that scenario last year at Poole – because he could have easily done it on the Zeebrugge-Hull one. Time bomb or something like that.'

The fat little man pursed his lips, brow wrinkled in thought. Outside the wind howled and lashed the snowflakes savagely against the windscreen. Now the screen was completely blocked with snow. All sound was muted. They could have been the last people alive in the world. 'All right,' he said finally, 'let's accept that–'

Before he could pose his question, Seal interrupted him and said, 'Sir, it's just struck me. This terrorist of ours, who has been on the terrorist scene for well over ten years, is leaving a trail behind him a yard wide. Is it intentional? Or is he out of practice and making elementary mistakes in covering up his tracks.' Seal forced a laugh. 'I mean it is slightly untidy leaving not one, but *two* dead bodies behind him in the last three days.'

The MI5 man whistled softly and said, 'I see what you mean. Seal, do you think I could have another sip of that excellent malt whisky of yours?'

'Of course, sir.' Dutifully Seal handed him the silver flask once more and he took a drink. Then the MI5 man said, 'It's almost as if he's intent on being caught ... as if' he sought for the right words, *'he was being set up.'*

'A fall guy,' Seal prompted him.

'A fall guy, if I may use an Americanism. The question is, Captain Seal, for whom?'

But Seal had no answer for that over-whelming question.

Half an hour later with the man from MI5 safely tucked away in his room in the great old Victorian former station hotel, Seal was listening on the telephone to the Brig's latest information gained from Daisy Cummings.

'So it is to be a rig. It'll be in the North Sea because the semtex was to be cached in that area and it'll be a British installation, not an American one. They are too well guarded. So, my dear Seal, it looks as if the ball is well and truly in the court of Team alpha.'

'I see, sir. Then we'll stay based here in Hull. But there's also, this, sir.' Swiftly he explained to the Brig his suspicions that he thought the Palestinian was a fall guy. Someone else was ensuring that he was being tracked to his objective.

He paused and there seemed to be a long silence at the other end of the line. Over on the billboards opposite the line of telephones, a notice read: *Government Facing Defeat over Europe again. Germans will take initiative*.

Finally the Brig broke the silence with, 'I feel you might be right. Therefore, we have to be prepared for a surprise from another quarter. All the same, our main priority is to ensure that this Palestinian chap is caught before he can put his plan, whatever it may be, into action. I think I shall now take over from Daisy and have a little word with this Aziz fellow myself.'

Seal bit his bottom lip. The Brig often played too hard. He hoped there'd be no trouble when he had his 'little word' with 'this Aziz fellow'. 'All right, sir,' he said. 'I'll await further orders.'

'You'll get them, never fear. Time is running out. We've got to get this chap soon, before it is too late.' Then the line went dead.

Thoughtfully Seal walked back through the blizzard to his waiting car. It was shrouded with snow again. He brushed it off with the side of his big hand, hardly aware he was doing so, his mind on other things.

Russia was out of the game now. She had too many internal problems. The Palestinians and the Israelis had roughly patched up their long standing quarrel. Neither of those two groups would be interested in damaging Britain. That left the Middle East. He thought of Iraq and the sheer naked hatred for the British his Republican Guard captors had shown him and the rest of the Alpha Team, during those awful twenty-four hours when they had been in Iraqi hands. He remembered the beatings, the terrible threats. Yes, some Iraqis would do anything to hurt Britain, especially to exact revenge for the defeat in the Gulf five years previously.

Suddenly his train of thought stopped. Barely glimpsed in the whirling snow, he spotted a dark figure working on the door handle of the next car to his, some ten yards away. The dark figure bent and worked and then cast a glance to left and right, as if looking for someone. Then he got it. It was a car thief trying to break into the black Astra.

He crossed the intervening distance, noiseless in the thick snow. He dropped his big hand on the little figure and said, 'Hey, what's going on here?'

The would-be car thief dropped the screwdriver he was holding in surprise and turned round.

Gosh, Seal said to himself. The car thief couldn't have been a day older than twelve. He was skinny and freckled, his face looking pale and sick under the tilted baseball cap. Aloud Seal said, 'Hey, what do you think you're up to?'

'What the fuck d'yer think?' the sick-looking boy sneered. 'I'm fucking well breaking into this fucking car.'

Seal was shaken by the child's audacity. 'Don't you know that's against the law?' he stuttered a little foolishly.

The boy sniggered. 'Are you the brain o' Britain, mister?' he mocked. 'Course it's against the fucking law.' He looked cockily through the falling snow at the big man. 'Tenth I've broken into this year.' He poked his thumb at his skinny chest. 'They can't do nowt about me, cos I'm underage.' He tugged the dewdrop from the end of his nose and flung it contemptuously into the snow. 'So fuck off.' He turned, as if to resume his break-in.

Seal clenched his fist menacingly. The boy caught the gesture. 'Go on, mister, why don't yer hit me,' he challenged Seal, a cocky look on his sick face. 'Have yer lost yer marbles? The coppers'd have you behind bars in a flash if yer hit me. I've told yer already, nobody can do nothing against me, cos–'

The rest of his words ended in a cry of pain as Seal hit him with the flat of his hand – hard. The skinny kid sailed right over the bonnet of the Astra and slammed into the deep snow on the other side. He stared up aghast at the big officer, mouth open in total disbelief, that this was happening to him.

'Under age, eh... Nothing can happen to you,' Seal said happily, feeling relieved of some of the tension from this frustrating winter's day. 'Seems you were wrong, sonny.'

Then he opened the door of his car and drove slowly away. Behind him, still lying in the deep snow, the would-be thief started to cry, moaning, *Mummy ... Mummy ... Mummy.'*

168

Chapter Five

The two young men in the thick overcoats, faces shaded by their cloth caps, were polite but firm. They fell in on both sides of Aziz, as he came out of the Tube, and said, 'Would you come this way, sir.' It wasn't a request though; it was an order.

'What ... what is this?' Aziz protested, his dark face suddenly flushing with fear.

'Just come along with us, sir,' the taller of the two said firmly. 'I'm sure you don't want any trouble.'

'But who are you ... what do you want ... where are you taking me?' the student stuttered, as they steered him purposefully to the car parked on a double yellow line, engine running, windscreen wipers ticking back and forth in the snow.

At the car door Aziz, realizing his danger for the first time, tried to make a break for it, but the bigger of the two was quicker. He grabbed Aziz's right arm and twisted it painfully behind his back. 'Let's do it nice and easy, sir,' he said calmly, though the menace in his voice was all too clear. He pushed Aziz into the back seat and followed him inside. Squeezed in between the two of them, Aziz could smell his own sweat; it stank of fear.

'Please tell me what's going on,' he quavered, near to tears. But as the big car moved into the mid-afternoon traffic, skidding and slithering in the snow which seemed never ending, the two of them remained obstinately silent.

Half an hour later Aziz found himself in the cellar of one of those surprisingly elegant Georgian houses still to be found in run-down, crime-ridden Camberwell. He had been left alone for a while and had cried. Now he had composed himself, his mind racing electrically, as he stared around the bare walls, with the marks where the eighteenth-century wine racks had once been.

Obviously this was in connection with the Palestinian; and obviously the men who had kidnapped him were some kind of police. They acted the part. That constant use of 'sir' gave them away. He sniffed and felt a little better. He knew the English police. They were racist all of them, but they kept strictly to the law. There would be none of the torture the police used in his own native country, So, he concluded, it would be a matter of question and answer. As he had not committed any crime, he couldn't see what they could do to him.

In all probability they would be the Special Branch – hence the unorthodox manner of arrest – but they'd stick to the rules of evidence, too.

All he had to do was to keep his head and not give too much away. After all, he was studying for a doctorate and they were flat-footed cops, who had probably left school at sixteen. His intellect should be able to cope with them. Thus it was that he was feeling in a much more confident mood when the door opened to admit the two kidnappers, followed a moment later by the tall im-posing figure with a military bearing who was much older.

They stared at the man on the chair in the circle of yellow light cast by the single naked bulb for what seemed a long time. Aziz suddenly began to feel uneasy. Perhaps the tales he had heard of the correctness of the British police weren't true. Perhaps they, too, had secret underground torture chambers, where the victims screams and pleas couldn't be heard, just like the police back home had. He licked his dry lips uneasily.

'Mr Aziz,' the old man broke the uneasy silence in soft, clipped tone, 'I'd like you to answer us a couple of quick questions. Then we'll let you get on your way, without any further delay.' He let his words sink in for a long moment.

Aziz felt only contempt for the softly spoken old man. What a bumble! In his own country the interrogator would have first stubbed out a cigarette on his cheek or smashed him in the teeth before even speaking a word. He waited with ever-growing confidence.

'We know,' the old man continued in that gentle tone of his, 'that you have some association with a terrorist organization linked to the Middle East. We know further, that you are aware of the whereabouts in this country of a former associate of the Jackal's, known as the Palestinian. Could you now please tell us what that organization is and where the Palestinian is, too?'

Inwardly Aziz smiled at the use of that 'please'. Outwardly he pretended rage. 'I know nothing about either,' he declared hotly. 'I'm a doctoral student at the London School of Economics – a serious man, who will soon be returning–'

His words ended in a howl of pain as one of the men guarding the door walked swiftly over to where Aziz sat and punched him hard in the nose. Blood started to pour from it, while the old man stared at him mildly, as if he couldn't understand what exactly was happening.

Aziz took out his handkerchief and held it to his nose. 'You can't do that to me,' he said thickly, the white handkerchief rapidly turning red with his own blood. 'I shall call the police.'

The old man said calmly, 'No police ever

come to this region, Mr Aziz. They've long given up on it. This place belongs to the drug dealers and the pimps. Here, you are beyond the law. This is a no-go area.'

Suddenly Aziz felt a cold finger of fear trace its way down the small of his back.

'Now then,' his interrogator's voice was brisker now, 'please let's get on with it. I asked you two questions, please be good enough as to answer them.'

Aziz began to protest that he didn't know, but he stopped short when he saw the taller of the two guards take out a pair of brass knuckles and begin slipping them carefully, almost lovingly, onto his right hand. The fight went out of him. 'It's President Hussein,' he said weakly. 'It is his revenge for the cowardly – er,' hastily Aziz changed his words, 'his revenge for the attack on Iraq five years ago.'

'And that revenge is to be?'

'Something to do with oil,' Aziz said. He saw the man with the brass knuckles frown and he stuttered hastily, 'May God be my witness, that is all I know.'

The old man nodded to the younger one

174

and the latter relaxed. 'Where?' he asked.

'Somewhere in the North Sea,' Aziz gulped and said hastily. The blood was dripping to his chin now and he felt he might well be sick.

'And your friends who will help this Palestinian – where are they located? Bradford, Leeds, Northampton, somewhere like that?' he prompted. Again the man with the brass knuckles frowned and looked impatient.

The prisoner looked at the guard and then the old man frantically. 'Honest, I don't know. Only up north. I don't think Bradford though,' he added hastily, as the guard slammed the brass knuckles into the palm of the other hand audibly.

'Perhaps Leeds?' the old man prompted.

Aziz shook his head swiftly. 'No, not Leeds. Too many Jews there with connections to the Mossad.' He licked his parched lips. 'That's all I know. Not Bradford and not Leeds.'

The old man seemed to consider. Then he turned and nodded to the husky young men at the door. They nodded back and suddenly, overcome with fear at the realization, Aziz knew they were not just going to take him away. Just like the secret police would do in his own country, they were going to silence him for good; *they were going to kill him!* He put up his hands in front of his face as if to blot out their images.

'Please don't kill me,' he quavered, tears trickling down his bloody cheek. 'If you don't kill me I shall tell you a great secret ... oh, please don't kill me ... please sir.' He sank to his knees, clutching and wringing his hands together in the classic pose of supplication.

The old man's face tensed suddenly. 'What did you say? A great secret. What great secret?' He rasped.

'It's connected with the German,' Aziz babbled, knowing now that he was fighting for his very life.

'*A German!*' the old man exclaimed. Obviously he had been caught completely off his guard. This was very clearly a surprising development for him. 'What has a German got to do with this affair?'

'It was an old comrade of the *Rote Armee*

*Fraktion,'** Aziz explained, still on his knees with the tears streaming down his face.

'But they disappeared from the terrorist scene years ago,' the old man objected.

'I know, I know, sir. But last month this old comrade approached us in London, gave us some money and asked about the Palestinian.'

'But what did this German want to know?'

'Just what the operation was and which rig had been–'

'What did you say?' the old man interrupted sharply.

Aziz cursed himself. He had let something slip. But it didn't matter now. He was fighting for his life. 'Which rig was to be attacked,' he admitted lamely.

'And you told?'

Aziz nodded numbly.

'Well, which one was it?'

'One belonging to UK Oil,' Aziz answered.

'A particular one?' At the door the taller of the two guards slammed the brass knuckles into his other palm once more.

* Red Army Fraction.

'I don't know that, honestly I don't,' Aziz answered hastily.

'All right, one last question. Did this German from the *Rote Armee Fraktion* know the Palestinian's route?'

'Yes, from Luxembourg to the Belgian coast, he did.'

The old man looked thoughtful and Aziz realized instinctively that his life had been saved. The information about the German had done the trick. Slowly and carefully he rose from his knees and the old man didn't object. Instead he nodded to the guards. They stalked forward and took Aziz by the arms. He'd spend the next two nights in a Special Branch Cell before he was quietly deported, instead of lying at the bottom of the Thames.

After he had gone the Brig stroked his chin thoughtfully. Now he knew how the Police in Luxembourg and Belgium had been able to follow the Palestinian's trail so easily. The German had informed on him. The Brig frowned and spoke to himself in the manner of lonely men, *'But who the hell is this damned German?'*

Chapter Six

They grabbed Jacko just as he was about ready to unlock the radio shack. They were Hurst, Big Slack and half a dozen of the others. It was dark now and they could no longer see the escaping gas erupting, but they could still hear the obscene noise the bubbles made when they burst on the surface – 'like a damn great elephant farting,' Big Slack had quipped.

'Hey, what's the frigging game!' Jacko cried in alarm, as they took hold of him and pulled the keys to the shack from his hand.

'Shut yer gob!' Hurst snapped and taking the first of the two keys needed to open the shack, stuck it in the security lock. Then he inserted the other one and the door opened to reveal the radio and the various other signalling devices.

'Move it,' Hurst shouted and Big Slack pushed the frightened little radio operator into the shack.

Jacko stumbled in, crying, 'You know you're not allowed–'

Big Slack punched him hard and he shut up.

'All right,' Big Slack cried, pushing him into his seat, 'I want you to raise the *Hull Daily Mail* by phone and tell 'em this.'

'But I've not got the number.'

'We have,' Big Slack replied and slapped an old copy of the local paper on the desk in front of a frightened Jacko. 'There you are. Get yer bleeding finger out and get cracking.'

'What will Red Ross say?' Jacko cried.

'Fuck Red Ross,' Big Slack said. 'We're giving the frigging orders now.' He took the piece of paper from his pocket on which they had pencilled their 'statement', as it was headed. He read it aloud one more time to check, 'We, the crew of the oil rig the *Margaret Thatcher*, are working under conditions that are potentially lethal.' He smiled. He liked those posh words that Hurst had dreamed up. 'If we was–'

'*Were*,' Hurst corrected him hastily.

'Were unionized, this would not be tolerated. Perhaps Mr Higgs of the–'

He never finished the statement. At that moment the door swung open and Red Ross flew in, eyes blazing with rage. He took in the scene in a flash. 'Why you rotten prick, Hurst!' he snorted, knowing instinctively that the man he had struck, was behind what was going on in the shack. 'You know you're forbidden to come in here.' He lashed out with a fist like a small steam shovel.

Hurst took the punch full in the face. He went reeling back, spitting out teeth, blood squirting from his broken lips. Big Slack clenched his fists. Red Ross didn't give him a chance to do anything. 'Fancy yer frigging luck, Slack Arse do yer?' Again his fist lashed out. It caught 'Slack Arse' in the stomach. He doubled up, gasping painfully for breath.

Red Ross glanced around their suddenly pale faces, panting for breath, his eyes flashing fire. 'Anyone else?' he demanded. 'Come on, I'll take the bloody lot of yer on, with one frigging fist tied behind my back if yer like!'

But there were no takers. Slowly Ross lowered his fists and said more calmly now, 'All right back to your mess.' He stared hard at Hurst. 'And you're off this rig as soon as the next chopper comes in. I'll make it my business personally to see you are blacked on every rig in the North Sea. You'll never work in the oil industry again.'

'But Red,' Hurst protested thickly through his swollen lips, 'I was only–'

'Fuck off!' Red Ross interrupted him and he slunk away with the rest, patting his bleeding lips.

Ross waited till they had gone. Then he reached into his pocket and brought out a small pistol. 'Used to have them with us all the time when we worked off South America.'

Jacko looked at the weapon aghast. 'But I don't know how to use a pistol, Red.'

'Easy. You pull the trigger and shoot the bugger. And that's what you do to anybody else who breaks in here. You're within rights as well.' He picked up the piece of paper the group had left behind, as Jacko explained they had wanted him to contact the *Hull*

Daily Mail. 'Blackmailing sods,' he snorted. 'Well, I'm not having that union sod telling me how I'm going to run my rig, no sir! I'd rather do all the jobs mesen than work with union labour–'

'Red,' Major Honor's voice cut into his words urgently.

He spun round. 'What is it, Major?'

'We're blowing a crater, Red,' the Major answered.

'Oh sweet Jesus.' Red clapped a big hand to his head like a man sorely tried. 'Not that!'

''Fraid so,' the Major answered and he could see from the look on Red Ross's face the latter knew as well as he did, what it meant. Sitting as they were, right in the middle of an oil field, they could expect another crater to open up underneath them at any moment. Then the four storey, twenty thousand ton rig could disappear as if it were some kid's meccano toy.

Jacko whistled softly and said in an awed voice, 'Hell's bells we could be swimming in the frigging North Sea before I had time to send out a "mayday"...'

Day Four:

Thursday

'The first generation of ruins, cleaned up, shored up began to weather – in the daylight they took their places as the norm of the scene... Reverses, losses, deadlocks, now almost unnoticed, bred one another; every day the news hammered one more nail into a consciousness which no longer resounded. Everywhere hung the heaviness of even worse, you could not be told and could not desire to hear. This was the lightless middle of the tunnel.'

Elizabeth Bowen: The Heat of the Day.
c 1942

Chapter One

Von Klarsfeld parked his Porsche, with a flourish and in a swish of new snow, in the special visitors' parking lot of UK Oil.

It was still snowing and although he had been born in Bavaria, where it snowed a lot, he could not recollect seeing so much snow in such a short time. And it wasn't the kind of snow he remembered from his Bavarian youth – pure white, crystalline and beautiful, set against a backdrop of white mountain peaks silhouetted in a perfect blue sky. This snow was heavy and angry, falling from a leaden sky against a backdrop of ugly high-rise buildings constructed in the Sixties. This snow seemed to typify England – ugly, sad, purposeless.

He reached in the back of the car for his green *Loden* coat that looked more like a cloak than a coat and his Bavarian hat with its *Federbusch*. Von Klarsfeld had spent two years at Eton and knew exactly what an upper class Englishman would have worn on a day like this. Instead he wore clothes that he realized made him look a caricature of a German. But that's why he wore them because he was a German and proud of being one. Perhaps in due course he would affect a monocle and complete the picture of what the English thought a Prussian should look like, though as a Bavarian he hated all *Saupreiss*. *

He reached in for his smart leather briefcase, engraved with the family coat of arms, fixed the wheel-locking devices –England was such a lawless country – and locked the Porsche.

He stamped through the new snow, back erect, head held high, very proud of himself and his country. 'And why shouldn't I be?' he asked himself as he approached the entrance to UK Oil. The old days of Germany eating humble pie, because of the war, were long over. Hitler's Third Reich

* Bavarian name for the Prussians, i.e. sow
  Prussians.

might have lost the military battle, but the survivor of Hitler's vaunted '1,000 Year Reich', the Common Market under Germany's leadership, had won the economic battle.

'My dear fellows,' he would tell English visitors to his Frankfurt office, 'what was the pound worth forty years ago? You don't know. Then I shall tell you. Twelve marks. What's it worth today? Barely *two* marks. That says it all, doesn't it, old chaps.' And he would laugh in that refined old Etonian manner as if it were all a splendid joke. But underneath there would be that old atavistic German *schadenfreude* and a little voice at the back of his head saying maliciously, 'That's telling 'em!'

He walked into the entrance, slapping the snow off his coat. The commissionaire snapped to attention, saluted and said, 'Good-morning, sir.'

Von Klarsfeld liked that. Germany could use a corps of commissionaires, too, but those damned 'greens' and all the rest of those parlour pinks who were against anything in uniform wouldn't wear it. 'Good-morning to you,' he answered with excessive heartiness. Then taking the key out of his pocket, he stepped to the executive lift and opened it.

Honor's secretary was waiting for him at the fifth floor. Obviously the commissionaire had alerted her to his arrival. In some ways he thought the English were quite efficient and their women were decidedly pretty, as this one was. 'Good-morning Baron,' Hilary Stevens said with a bright smile.

He looked at her splendid breasts, two firm mounds tilting upwards, the nipples clearly visible through the thin material of her blouse, breasts just waiting to be sucked, he thought to himself. 'Good-morning ... er ...'

'Stevens, sir ... Hilary Stevens, sir,' she volunteered, reaching out to take his coat.

'Thank you,' he said, brushing against her left breast, as she took the garment and feeling a sense of sexual excitement. 'I popped by today to find out what the latest is on the "Iron Maiden",' he laughed. 'You know the *Margaret Thatcher?*'

Hilary Stevens frowned to herself. She wished she knew. Aloud she said, 'We've had nothing from the rig for the last twenty-four hours, sir.'

'That's strange,' he said, taking a cigarette out of his cigarette case, German, of course, a *Lord*. These days he wore only German clothes, smoked German cigarettes – he had even given up scotch for schnaps or Asbach-Uralt, the German brandy. 'You'd have thought that the – er – Major would have wanted to report in any progress they've made out there.'

She didn't respond. She didn't like the Baron and somehow she felt it strange that he was prepared to make the journey across snowbound London to ask his question when he could have done it more easily by fax or telephone from his suite in The Savoy. He must have read her mind, for the next moment von Klarsfeld said, 'The real reason I came over was to see you.'

'*Me?*' Hilary Stevens flushed prettily.

He liked that. He preferred his women to appear, at least, to be naïve and innocent. His wife, the Baroness, was far too sophisticated for him. With her, sex had to be so complicated and it took her hours before she would moan, *'ich spende ... ich spende!'* His mistress in Frankfurt was much easier in that area, but he suspected that when he was absent she had other men. Once he had actually caught her yawning when he had gone down on her as a great favour.

'Yes,' he continued, 'I thought you might like to come to lunch. I've booked a table at the Gay Hussar. I know it's always full of left-wing politicians, and that old lord who's always waffling on about prisoners, but they serve the kind of food and portions you can get back home in Germany. Goulash, that kind of stuff.' He smiled winningly at her.

'But I've brought my sandwiches, sir,' she said, somewhat stupidly.

His smile broadened, but the blue eyes remained steely and hard. 'Feed 'em to the pigeons. Just regard it as a working lunch, that's all. After all, you know as much about the Major's intentions as anyone, being his private, confidential secretary.'

She flushed even more and he wondered why.

She, for her part, thought he might have known something had gone on between Justin and herself. All the same, she realized that there was something else behind the Baron's motives. So, quite surprisingly, she heard herself saying in a flirty kind of way, 'Thank you, kind sir, I shall be honoured.'

'I, too. Good. I shall pick you up at twelve-thirty precisely.' And with that he was gone, striding importantly into the directors' board room, leaving her to stare at his back in deep thought.

Chapter Two

Red Ross stared round the circle of worried unshaven faces under the yellow hard hats. 'All right, lads,' he bellowed against the noise from outside. 'I know yer scared that another one of them bloody gas holes might open up underneath the rig. I'm scared mesen. But I've been in this bloody business thirty years or more now and I've never known it happen underneath a rig. All the same me and the Major,' he indicated a weary, dirty-faced Honor standing next to him, 'have decided to offer each of you fifty extra quid danger money, no matter what yer trade or skill, each day, till you end your shift. I reckon that'll be an extra three hundred nicker for every one of yer.'

'Don't listen to him,' Hurst mumbled at the back of the group of workers. 'What's three hundred quid worth when you're at the bottom of t'North Sea, mates?'

Red Ross gave him a look of contempt and said, 'A couple of gas bubbles bursting like wet farts shouldn't scare a bunch of hairy-arsed oilmen like you lot, think of it, three hundred quid. When you go off shift, yer can get the dirty water off yer chest with them Hull tarts for a whole weekend with that kind of money. At thirty quid a throw yer'll be able to jump ten o' them, that is those of yer who ain't funny.' He made the limp wrist gesture and some of them laughed.

It worked. The rebellion had been beaten. Hurst kicked a metal pail across the floor of the rig in frustrated rage but as the men drifted away to their tasks, chatting excitedly about the further bonus, he, too, went back to his job.

Honor looked at Red Ross, who was breathing hard, as if he had just run a hard race. Back in Korea all those years before, he told himself, Ross would have made an ideal NCO: one of those types who were unflappable, knew their men and always managed to get the best of them, whatever the circumstances, an NCO who could talk the men's language better than any officer. Thank God, he thought, Britain still produced men like Red Ross. They were the salt of the earth.

'Thanks Red,' he said when Ross had recovered.

'Don't mention it,' he answered. 'All part of the job. But Major, what we need now is luck. It just can't go on like this. Gas leaks, craters, fouled-up equipment.' He clenched his fist aggressively. 'We've just got to find that bloody oil by the end of this shift. I don't think we can stand the strain much longer.'

Justin Honor laid his hand on the big foreman's muscular shoulder. 'We will Red... *We must!*'

Now despite the weather and the snowstorm howling in straight from Siberia, the terrible race to find oil before the money ran out went on. As the drill bit deeper into the hard rock of the sea's beds, beneath the tossing grey-green surface of the sea, the whole rig seemed to tremble like a live thing. In the galleys mugs and plates fell to the floor. On the platforms loose bits of gear clattered back and forth and those working on the outer edges, had to hang on to stanchions to keep from being thrown into the sea so far below.

Now Red Ross was driving the men with all his tremendous energy, not sparing himself, not even pausing for that 'mug o'char' that his big body craved for. Around him the floormen worked in impossible conditions, the spray and snow streaming down their yellow oilskins, their faces brick-red and chapped in the freezing, fierce wind. But Red Ross didn't seem to notice. The slightest stoppage and he was on to the workman concerned, berating him with a flood of obscenities.

But the men didn't mind. For the first time since the *Margaret Thatcher* had become operational, they were caught up in the excitement, the adventure of it all. Dripping with seawater, their oilskins mud-stained to the thigh, chests heaving with almost unbearable strain, they staggered back and forth with the steel pipe needed for the drill. All that mattered now was – *to find oil!*

Above the workers, the arc lights swung back and forth crazily. The derrick moaned. The wind braces shrieked. Down below, the sea attacked the rig time and time again, as if attempting to deny them their prize. But the drilling did not cease.

A chain being used to haul up a part snapped. It whipped through the air lethally, scattering mud to left and right. Red Ross launched himself forward in a flying tackle. Hurst went flying to the deck in the same instant that that massive steel whip sliced the air where he had just been standing.

'You all right, Hurst?' Red Ross asked, breathing hard.

'Sure,' Hurst said, rising to his feet a little unsteadily. 'Missed me by miles ... and thanks, Red.'

Ross blushed.

A few minutes later he said to Honor, 'Did you see that, Major? Twenty-four hours ago and something like that would have had the whole bunch laying down their tools. Now we've got them. For the first time since we started operations on the *Margaret Thatcher,* we've got 'em, Major.'

Honor responded to the foreman's enthusiasm. 'You're right, Red. They're behind us now. And you know what?' He stared hard at the other man, 'I have a gut feeling that our luck has changed. We're going to do it this time...'

It was about then that Jacko called them into the radio shack with, 'message from head office in London, sir.'

Honor grinned happily. They all knew where head office was, but Jacko always liked to make things sound important.

It was Hilary. Although her voice was distorted by static he could still hear her sense of shock and the worry, as she said, 'I've just had lunch with the Baron ... and, sir, I think something funny is going on.'

'Funny?' he echoed. 'How funny?'

The Gay Hussar was busy, as always. The usual bald-headed lord was sitting at the table near the entrance, deep in discussion with a man with ear rings. Inside the place was full of politicians, some of them with their latest books which, in due course, would be placed on display on the shelf above their heads. The place smelled of power and privileges.

The Baron guided her to the table, leading the way in the German fashion, while the waiters, who obviously knew von Klarsfeld, bowed and scraped and rubbed their hands, as if in anticipation of a large tip.

It was half-way through the meal and well into the second bottle of Tokay, which he had ordered and of which he had drunk the most, and with his hand lightly resting on her right knee under the table, that he had started to talk. First it had been about her. 'You see I'm thinking of transferring quite a lot of my operations to London, dear,' he had said, pressing her knee. 'The Deutsche and Dresdner Banks have moved there. So it would be handy to be close to their international dealers and perhaps,' he had licked his lips and had looked into her eyes knowingly, 'you might like to come and – er – *work* for me.' He had emphasized the word significantly.

Then he had pressed her knee once more and she had known what he had meant by 'work'.

'Of course, there would be a substantial increase in salary and I would provide a cosy little flat for you in the centre. Make it easier for you to get to work, avoiding that horrid London Tube of yours. God knows what kind of gross bugs one picks up in a place like that.'

She had said nothing, just listened. Once, however, when he had tried to push his hand up between her thighs, she had thrust it away, but he hadn't seemed to notice. She suspected he was quite drunk.

'I think you could be quite a help to me. You know the inner workings of the business through collaborating with Major Honor – curious name that,' he had added and chuckled a little stupidly so that the Labour politician sitting at the next table turned and stared at him.

Then recognizing the Baron, he said loudly to the companion, 'Did you see that headline in *The Times* about the Dresdner Bank – "First the Tank, then the Dresdner Bank". They meant during the war, first the German military went in and then the Dresdner Bank to make a profit out of the

Nazi conquests.'

Baron von Klarsfeld flushed angrily. 'No one ever said that in Germany in those days, because in German the words simply do not rhyme.'

The Labour politician didn't react, but continued drinking his bottle of Château de Rothschild.

'Where was I?' Klarsfeld asked, face flushed now with both anger and drink.

'You said I could be quite a help to you,' she prompted, 'In what way?' She looked at him curiously and pushed his hand away as it started to wander up above her stocking tops once more. She knew already what he wanted, but there was something else there, too, she realized.

'Well, you see,' he said a little hesitantly, as if he were finding it difficult to formulate his words, 'I should think I might be asked to take over if anything goes wrong with the *Margaret Thatcher*.'

'You mean if the rig doesn't find oil?' she prompted.

'Not exactly that. Our geologists tell us there's plenty of oil down there. Otherwise we wouldn't have backed the project in the first place. No.' He frowned and took another hefty swig at his wine before continuing. 'Oil *will* be found in due course. There is no doubt about that. No, what I mean is if some disaster overtakes the rig.' He said the words in a hurry as if he was glad to get them off his chest at last.

She stared at him aghast. 'Some disaster. What kind of a disaster?'

Suddenly he was embarrassed. 'Oh, you know, my dear,' he blustered, even taking his hand off her knee as he did so. 'So many things can go wrong on those structures – explosions, helicopter crashes...'

'And then he mentioned terrorism, Major,' Hilary said.

'What?' the Major asked, wondering if he had heard Hilary correctly.

'Terror-ism!' she shouted back over the phone and this time he knew he had heard her correctly.

'In what context did he say that?'

'That he might have to take over in case some disaster struck,' she answered. 'He mentioned explosions, chopper crashes and the like. Then he said in case of a terrorist attack.'

'Anything else?' Honor asked swiftly.

'No. By then he was obviously half seas over and he started to attempt to pull himself together – black coffee and all that. I couldn't get anything else out of him.'

'All right. Thank you, Hilary. You've done a splendid job. I'll make up for it when I return to London.' For a moment he had a vision of her naked young body, as she had stepped out of her knickers and had stood there awkwardly. It had been one of the most beautiful moments of his life. He shook his head and made himself forget that last afternoon. 'Look after yourself, Hilary, and keep me posted.'

'I will,' she breathed at the other end. 'Love you.' The phone went dead.

Chapter Three

The Palestinian found the house without too much difficulty. It was not far from the station and the railway line ran in front of it. Once, he supposed the area had been a prosperous middle class suburb. Now it had been taken over by B and Bs and students' digs. The house had been run down all right. There were no curtains on the windows, the frames of which hadn't been painted for years and there were dirty empty milk bottles on the bare table he could see through the window.

He stepped over a pile of fresh dog turds, wrinkling his nose as he did so and glanced at the long list of occupants. This was the right place, he told himself. They were all his own people.

He rang the bottom bell. It was the room belonging to 'George' as they had code-named him back in Baghdad. After a while he could hear a shuffling down the corridor, the security chain was taken off and the door opened.

A dark, hook-nosed figure stood there, a book in his hand, pencil stuck behind his right ear. He looked as if he had just been taking notes from the textbook. 'Yes?' he asked without interest, dark eyes sullen, as if he resented being disturbed. Outside a train thundered by and the wind from it whipped the clothes around their bodies.

'George?' he asked.

George's face was suddenly animated. His dark eyes flashed. '*You?*' he asked excitedly.

He nodded.

George took his hand in both of his and gushed, 'Come on in, I've heard so much about you. You were one of my heroes even when I was still in short pants.' Hurriedly he urged the Palestinian into the dirty, smelly hallway, steering him by the rusty old cycles and a large rucksack with the notice printed on it, '*Do not touch. This rucksack will self-destruct*'. The Palestinian was not amused. He had seen too many lethal devices in his time which actually did that.

George opened the door to his room, which was just as dirty and untidy as the rest of the house, and ushered the Palestinian inside. 'You will take tea?'

'Later,' the Palestinian said and sat on a broken chair which creaked alarmingly. 'Tell me the set-up. Who have you got?'

'There are four whom you can rely on one hundred per cent,' George answered, 'and we have a few more prepared to help if it isn't too risky.'

'The four will suffice. Go on.'

'There's a problem, though.'

'What?'

'The Semtex hasn't arrived. Yesterday we searched the spot off Spurn Point where the German was supposed to deposit it. Not a sign.' George looked at the other man in a worried fashion, as if he expected abuse for his failure.

The Palestinian took it calmly. 'There will be other ways. All those rigs carry explosives as it is.'

'A change of plan. We board the rig then?' George asked eagerly, his dark eyes glowing in anticipation.

'Yes,' the Palestinian said carefully. Out-side another train raced by and the window rattled noisily. 'The rest of the plan, the approach method etc, remains the same. But we must board the rig, set the charges and destroy it. That is the order I was given by President Hussein and that is the order I will carry out.'

'Of course, of course,' George agreed hurriedly. 'We must show these English pigs that Saddam Hussein has a very long arm. One day when we have perfected our missiles, it will be the turn of New York.'

The Palestinian nodded. 'But first the *Margaret Thatcher* will have to suffice. It will be a symbol that will be understood throughout the Middle East. It will also show this third-rate little country that there is no hope for them.' The Palestinian's eyes glowed fanatically. 'Their old sources of oil have almost run out. Now we show them that we can destroy their new sources at will. It will show that England is finished for good!'

'Good ... good,' George cried joyously. 'I hate them, the English. How I hate them!

Now we shall ruin them, comrade.'

Outside another train rushed by, rattling the windows so much that the dirty curtains flew back and forth, and unable to speak, the two men sat facing each other in silent rapture...

They set out that afternoon in George's beaten-up old camping bus. Besides George and the Palestinian, there were two others he had selected, code-named Harry and Dick. They were not of the same race as he and George, but they were loyal and capable and they would, the Palestinian thought, do the job required of them. Now with the snowflakes hitting the old bus's window like tracer, they rolled eastwards towards the coast down the slick, treacherous roads.

The Palestinian didn't like snow, and he worried a little about the careless way that George drove, but he reasoned that the student was used to snow after several years spent in this accursed England, and, of course, the snowstorm would afford them the cover they needed.

They drove the dead straight Roman road

to Driffield, with the snow pelting down and hardly another vehicle on the road, till they reached the Yorkshire market town. Here, Dick who was doing the map-reading, raised his sulkily handsome face from his Collins Road Atlas and directed, 'We turn right here till we reach the railway station and there we turn left and head for Skipsea.'

'Thank you,' the Palestinian said with unusual politeness for him.

Dick flushed with pleasure. He, too, knew the Palestinian's reputation.

The Palestinian smiled at the handsome boy and then they were through Driffield, heading now for the coast along the road that ran parallel to the canal which led to the sea. For a while, they rode in silence till the Palestinian said, 'Operation Stormwind commences tomorrow morning, comrades.'

George almost took his hands off the wheel with excitement. *'Tomorrow!'* he exclaimed. The others were equally excited.

'Yes, tomorrow evening President Hussein will announce the news over Radio Baghdad. It will be all over the world within the hour,' the Palestinian continued. 'When the West and their treacherous allies, the Kuwaiti, attacked us five years ago, they called their operation – Desert Storm. Well then they sowed the seed. Now they are going to reap the whirlwind. Everyone will know that Operation Stormwind is the direct answer to the Americans' vaunted Desert Storm.' He nodded his head as if in approval.

For a while they discussed the operation, even forgetting the driving snow and the dangerously slick country road, but then as the prehistoric castle of Skipsea came into view and Dick began to direct them to the caravan site which would be their base for this night, all of them concentrated on the task in hand.

They drove down the deserted track that led to the site, wheels churning up a white wake of snow behind them. George who had done the initial reconnaissance said, 'There is a caretaker, but he lives in the village. There'll be no one on the site at this time, especially in this kind of weather.'

The Palestinian grunted something and stared at the sea through a gap in the storm.

It was green and angry with the waves flecked white, as they slammed into the mud cliffs of the place. He hoped the weather would be better on the morrow.

George changed down gear, saying, 'I thought that caravan opposite the shop,' he indicated a brick building now shuttered up for the winter, 'would be our best bet. It seems to have several heaters.' He shuddered for it was cold in the van. 'Which would be useful in awful weather like this.'

The Palestinian nodded his approval. He eyed the building and made his decision. 'Let's stop the van. To the rear of the caravan.'

George did as he was ordered so that the van was concealed from the direction of the track. Then they got out, shivering in the cold, as the wind from the sea lashed the snowflakes into their dark faces.

For a moment the Palestinian eyed the caravan, its roof heavy with snow. The door, he saw, was easy. He could force it in a couple of seconds. He pulled out his knife and slid the blade in between the lock and the jamb.

He grunted, as he exerted pressure. A moment later and the door flew open. 'All right, let's get inside out of this snow,' he ordered.

They needed no urging. Hurriedly they piled into the flimsy structure, patting the snow off their clothes, slapping their arms about their bodies to get warm, while George knelt and turned on the electric fire. It worked. Gratefully they extended their frozen hands to the single bar.

It was just then that they were surprised by the gruff voice growling. 'Now then, what the hellus d'yer think yer up tier?'

They swung round, as one.

A tall man, muffled in an Army surplus greatcoat, with several buttons missing, was standing there challengingly in the flying snow – and he had a shotgun cocked over his right arm.

The Palestinian's brain raced electrically. It was clear that the man wasn't afraid of them on account of his shotgun. He had to be some sort of watchman and presumably he assumed they were the usual bunch of squatters who broke into caravans and the like in winter when they were unattended to get a roof over their heads. 'We didn't mean anything, mister,' he whined, as he had heard down-and-out Englishmen whine when he had been a student at the LSE so long before. 'Just trying to get in out of the cold.'

The big watchman sniffed, a look of contempt on his tough, unshaven face. 'Well, yer not bloody well doing it here, mate,' he answered. 'Come on ... off yer go. Hook it!' He paused. 'You're some kind o' foreigner, ain't you, mate.'

It was then that the Palestinian knew that he had to kill the watchman. His hand dropped to the pocket where the knife, with which he had opened the door of the caravan lay. 'All right, we're off,' he said, not answering the other man's question.

The three others looked at him.

The watchman moved to one side to let them come out. George, looked puzzled at the way the Palestinian had given in so tamely, and went out first. Harry and Dick followed. Then it was the Palestinian's turn. As he came close to the watchman, the latter said, 'And I've got the number of yer van. I'll be passing it onto the police. They can make you pay for what you did to that lo–'

The words died on his lips, as the Palestinian thrust the knife into his fat stomach and ripped it up savagely. His mouth flopped open stupidly and the shotgun fell from suddenly nerveless finger. 'What–'

The Palestinian grabbed him by the hair and pulled hard. His head came back, exposing the neck with a prominent Adam's apple. Carefully, taking his time, as if he were enjoying the whole thing, while the others watched in horrified fascination, he drew the knife slowly, cutting the man's throat from ear to ear, with the bright red blood dropping to the snow in great wet gobs.

He smiled thinly at them, knowing they would follow him anywhere now, and let the dead man drop noiselessly into the snow. He wasn't even breathing hard when he said, 'Just let's cover him with snow. That should do. We'll be gone by the morning.'

He bent and calmly wiped the blade of his
knife on the dead man's greatcoat. Then he
went inside to the warmth of the caravan
and let them get on with it.

218

Chapter Four

Seal listened attentively, as the Brig told him the latest in that crisp, clipped, precise manner of his. 'So we've been tapping the phones at UK Oil since the beginning of the week. Now we know that one of their money men, a German named von Klarsfeld, knows more than is good for him. He has hinted at an attack – a disaster, he called it. And we know where this disaster is going to strike. It's UK Oil's newest rig, the *Margaret Thatcher.*'

Seal grinned despite the seriousness of the situation. 'Poor Mrs Thatcher, she does come in for a lot of stick.'

At the other end of the line in London, the Brig ignored the comment. Instead he said, 'So now we have all the information we need. The attacker and his objective.' His optimistic tone vanished for a moment, as he added, 'Everything, except when the

Palestinian is going to attack.'

'Exactly, sir,' Seal agreed.

'At all events, the Navy has been alerted through friends and your commander is withdrawing his units in the Channel etc., and sending them north. But it'll be a day before they reach the North Sea. So my dear fellow, it looks as if it's up to you if our friend strikes before then.'

'Well, sir, there are only two ways that they can get at the *Margaret Thatcher* – by air or by sea.'

'Agreed. But the North Sea is very large, remember that. At events I want you to stand by. The RAF is going to place a people's pod at your disposal just in case. You've heard of them, haven't you?'

'Yessir.' Seal had. The 'people's pod' was a torpedolike tank placed beneath the wing of a Harrier jump jet. It could be used to carry troopers in on secret missions and the like. They were still at the experimental stage. But they had been already used in Bosnia, though Seal did not like the idea of being cooped up in a windowless tube of twenty-one feet in length and about two and a half feet in height and width.

'You don't sound as if you like that idea much,' the Brig said.

'A bit claustrophobic sir, without windows,' Seal replied honestly.

'The latest pod has got portholes, they tell me. But if this terrorist chap does slip through our net, it's the people's pod which is going to get you to the scene of the action in double quick time. All right, my friend, that's it for the time being.' The phone went dead.

Seal sat back in his armchair in the little hotel which housed the Alpha Team and rubbed his jaw. The Brig had done well. Still he didn't like the idea of the Harrier pod. He hoped it wouldn't come to that. It was no fun being cooped up under the wing of a jet going all out, knowing that if anything happened to the Harrier the men in the pod didn't stand a chance in hell of getting out. There were no ejector seats for them.

He dismissed the thought. For a while he tried to put himself in the place of the Palestinian. At the moment, since the semtex had been seized on the illegals' ship,

221

he would have no source of explosive, though he suspected the Palestinian might be able to get some elsewhere and there was always some on the rigs. They all carried explosives. But how was he going to get to the rig? More importantly, how was he going to leave it once the mission had been completed?

He thought for a while, wishing he could be like the rest of the Alpha Team who would probably be now in the hotel's little bar, downing beer, leaving their thinking up to him. But he knew he had to persist so he would be ready for anything that might come up – and be ready to act accordingly and at once.

The Brig had said the terrorist would strike either from the air or the sea. But if he used air, how would he get off the rig? Once the balloon went up, the sky would be swarming with British planes. Seal shook his head, looking at his determined young face in the wardrobe mirror. No, he wouldn't use the air; it would be the sea.

He got up from the chair and strode over to the little map of the East Yorkshire coast he had pinned onto the bedroom wall. Outside it was snowing once again and he could hear the snowflakes pelting against the wind. For a moment he was glad he was in a nice warm room on an evening like this.

With his forefinger he traced the coastline off which lay the *Margaret Thatcher,* some eighteen miles out to sea. Hornsea, Bridlington, Flamborough, Scarborough, Filey. He sniffed thoughtfully. Hornsea had no harbour. Neither did Filey. So they were both out of the question, as far as boats were concerned. He stared at the little hamlet of Flamborough. There were a couple of fishing boats there – cobbles, the locals called them – and the lifesavers' craft. He shook his head. No, he didn't think it could be Flamborough. 'That leaves Scarborough and Bridlington,' he mused aloud. Both were fishing ports and both had scores of small private boats moored in their harbours. Both, too, were within easy reaching distance of the rig. But which one was it?

Seal frowned at himself in the mirror. In

essence, he reasoned, there was little Alpha Team could do at the moment. There were only four of them after all, and they couldn't patrol two harbours which were a dozen miles apart from one another. He shrugged. Once the rest of the SBS teams were up north, then it would be different. They'd have enough men to cover both places.

Till then, he told himself, they'd have to cross their fingers and pray the terrorist wouldn't strike within the next twenty-four hours. He yawned and thought he'd better make an early night of it. Tomorrow would be a long day, somehow or other he knew that...

Two hundred miles away in London, the Brig, too, was tired, but he knew he wouldn't sleep even if he went to bed now. His mind was too active.

He knew that Seal and his Alpha Team would be quite capable of taking any necessary action once the balloon went up. But there were several imponderables which worried him. What role exactly was the

German von Klarsfeld playing in this matter? Surely the German wouldn't want anything to happen to the rig into which his backers had invested so much cash?

He had known, ever since Germany had become reunified five years or so before, that the country would start throwing its weight around. After all, Germany was the most powerful and the richest country in Western Europe. But it did have a basic weakness – no national source of energy and the Greens in that country were so powerful that they could ensure Germany's energy needs would not be supplied by nuclear power. No, the only secure source of energy, which couldn't be interrupted by political troubles as in Russia or Islamic fundamentalists as in the Middle East, was in the North Sea.

Was the German after control of the *Margaret Thatcher* and the other new rigs which would follow her once she had struck oil, and not just participation in the British venture? What in heaven's name was going on?

But before the Brigadier had time to

ponder that question any further, the phone at the table to his right rang. It was Daisy Cummings and she sounded both high and excited. 'I've found out something, sir,' she said hurriedly.

'What?'

'It's about the Palestinian. Now that Aziz has – er – gone, I've taken up with his pal, Hussein. I let him dick me this afternoon to get him talking.'

'Daisy,' the brigadier snapped, 'you mustn't use such terrible expression!'

Daisy Cummings chuckled and he knew now that she was on drugs again. 'Anyway, afterwards,' she continued, 'he started talking and told me that he's being sent to the north as a backman, as he called it. He meant a backup man. God, how some of those people get into university with their standard of English–'

'Carry on Daisy,' he interrupted her firmly. When she was high, Daisy tended to go off on a tangent.

'Well the bloke he was to contact in the north was code-named George, which doesn't help us much. Nor could he give me much of a description of this George, usual wog student type, Islamic fundamentalist sort of thing. However he did give me one damned good lead.'

'What?'

'Thought that would interest you, sir,' Daisy gushed.

'This George drives a Ford transit van converted into a kind of camper. Hussein's going off by train tonight, heading north. It will be his job to drive away the van when the others set off on what he called their "sacred mission".'

'He does seem to have told you a lot of information.'

'He was stoned and trying to be a big macho man – little streak of piss. But now they think I'm one of them, since most of them have been through me.'

Again the Brigadier shook his head in despair at her language but said nothing to interrupt her.

'So, sir, if you can get into the police computer, they might be able to identify the van for you.'

'Yes, you're right. But tell me one thing.

Did you find out this chap's destination?'

'No, he was suddenly very coy about that. But I do know he's just taken the tube to King's Cross, so that tells us he's using the East Coast line and when he had gone, I had a quick shufti around that pigsty he calls a room.'

'And?' the Brigadier asked expectantly.

'I found a map of Northern England and Bridlington, wherever that is up there in the wilds, was underlined in red. I checked quickly. You can still get a train from York to Bridlington. They haven't closed the line yet.'

'Super!' the Brigadier exclaimed with unusual enthusiasm for him. 'I think we've got it all about tied up, Daisy, thanks to you.' Then his voice grew calmer and more concerned. 'Daisy, you've done your bit for the time being. Can't we get out of this sordid business for a while and try to get you – what do they say – dried out?'

She laughed hollowly at the other end. 'You've got the expression right. But you've got the wrong bird, I'm afraid, sir. There's no hope for me. I'm hooked. Over, as we used to say in the old days.'

'Daisy, I'm sure,' he began, but then realized it was hopeless. The phone had gone dead.

Chapter Five

It was now nearly midnight. In the caravan the heat was nearly stifling. Outside there was no sound save the crash and thunder of the waves, slamming the mud cliff twenty-five yards away. They might well have been the last men alive in the world.

George brushed the empty cans which had contained their evening meal onto the already littered floor. The Palestinian frowned, for he liked neatness and order, but said nothing. Instead he smiled warily at Dick who lounged on the bunk bed opposite, clad only in his shirt and underpants. They were made of some kind of silken material and emphasized the bulge at the top of his muscular hairy legs. Angrily he tore his gaze away from that provocative bulge.

'So one last time,' the Palestinian said.

The other two bent their heads to listen

but Dick continued to look at him in undisguised admiration. The Palestinian sensed his blood racing. He controlled himself with difficulty. Sweat poured down his body. Allah, he prayed, let me control myself.

'You George, you begin,' he ordered.

'The Royal Air Force, the same one that bombed our innocent brothers in Baghdad in 1990,' George began bitterly, 'runs one of its search-and-rescue craft into Bridlington on every second day of the week. It is there to help pilots who come down into the North Sea and in summer for the pilot seaborne training exercises. The launch is due in again tomorrow.'

The Palestinian nodded and turned to the one codenamed 'Harry'. 'Continue,' he commanded.

Harry took up the second briefing. 'It will tie up just beyond the fish dock for three hours till low tide starts, before it moves out to sea...'

The Palestinian hardly heard the words. Dick was still watching, a smile on his dark handsome face. Was it possible, he asked himself, that he might be like that? He bit his bottom lip. In Allah's name why had *he* to be like this?

'At this time of the year,' Harry was saying, 'it will still be dark when the RAF launch takes up its position in the harbour. The fishing fleet will already be out to sea, so with luck, we might only have to cope with casual passersby – and in this weather, comrades, I don't think we'll have many of those. After all, this is what the English call – brass ape weather.'

The others laughed softly at the English expression in the midst of the flow of Arabic.

'So,' the Palestinian took up the briefing, 'as I have said before, the launch has a crew of five. As far as we know they are not armed – why should, they be in peacetime. We, on the other hand, are armed and have the advantage of surprise on our side. So let me repeat this to you, young comrades. There are two elements which will make a success of Operation Stormwind – speed and surprise.' He said the words again emphasizing them, '*Speed and surprise.* The slightest hesitancy and we might be lost. All right,' he looked at his watch, 'we shall leave here at five. That will allow us ample time to get in position behind the fishdock. Any questions?'

There were none.

He forced a little smile, trying not to look directly at that swelling bulge concealed by the silken material. 'Let me wish you all good luck, comrades.'

'Good luck to you, comrade,' the answers came back dutifully.

'Thank you. Now I shall put out the light. We wake up precisely at four-thirty. Is that clear?

'Clear.'

'Good, sleep!'

'Good luck, comrade.' It was Dick. As he clicked off the light in the caravan, Dick reached down from the upper bunk bed and pressed his hand. The young student's flesh was soft and warm like that of a woman's.

The Palestinian felt his blood race. 'Sleep,' he commanded again through gritted teeth.

Like trained soldiers, they turned in their bunks obediently and prepared to sleep.

But the Palestinian couldn't sleep. He still felt that soft touch, his mind filled with the thought of that terrible but delightful silken bulge. He thrust his fist into his mouth to prevent himself from moaning. All his life he had fought that shameful desire. Even now when he was old and mature it took a conscious effort of naked will-power to stop himself from reaching up to touch the handsome young man who slept above him, unaware of how the man below desired him. No, he ordered himself, this must stop. You must not bring shame upon yourself.

In the end he conquered himself. The desire ebbed and his breathing became normal. His heart began to beat normally. He turned and drew the rough woollen blanket about his head. Outside the wind from the sea howled and buffeted the caravan, making it tremble like a live thing. He did not notice. He lay in this dark, secret place and all was well once more.

Day Five

Friday

'We are the unwilling
Doing the unpleasant
For the ungrateful.'
*Doggerel circulating in
British Army Barracks in Ulster*

Chapter One

It was still snowing hard. This time the Palestinian was thankful for the falling snow. It gave them the cover they needed. Thirty minutes before, the last of Bridlington's fishing fleet had sailed for the fishing ground. Now the quay and the promenade behind were empty, the little seaside town still shrouded in sleep.

The others still sheltered in the van, complaining about the snow, the cold, the stink of rotting fish coming from the fish market sheds. But the Palestinian had ventured outside and, squinting against the falling snowflakes, he surveyed the sea the best he could.

Up on the promenade behind him, a paperboy pushing his bicycle, empty bag over his shoulder, slogged his way through the new snow, off to collect his papers for his round. He took no notice of the man next to the van. Perhaps he hadn't even seen him.

The Palestinian took his eyes off the sea and looked at his watch. The comrade from London who would collect and dump the van would arrive in half an hour. By then he hoped they'd be on their way. For now everything depended upon split-second timing. For the boat from Germany, which would pick them up, would only wait for two hours off the rig after they had completed their task. The spokesman for the mysterious German, who had financed most of the operation, had been very definite about that back in Baghdad when they had first started planning.

Suddenly he spotted the riding lights. There it was – their boat! Without taking his eyes off the faint bobbing lights, he rapped on the side of the van with his knuckles. They came tumbling out immediately, patting their pockets to check that they had their pistols.

'There she is,' the Palestinian hissed softly, as if he was afraid that someone might hear him.

Next to him the one code-named 'Dick' said excitedly, 'One day I shall be able to tell my grandchildren about this – what we did for the cause, eh, comrade.' He beamed up at the Palestinian.

At the back of the latter's head a harsh little voice rasped, 'If you live to have any grandchildren.' Aloud he said, 'Let's complete the operation first, comrade.'

'Yes, of course, comrade,' Dick agreed, a little crestfallen.

Now the yellow-painted launch, with the roundels of the RAF on its side, was approaching the green winking light of the harbour entrance. The watchers tensed. For all of them save the Palestinian, this was the first time they had ever done anything of this kind. Suddenly they were all aware that if anything went wrong, they could end up behind bars or even dead.

The Palestinian seemed to sense the change for he said sharply, 'Just carry out the orders as planned. Nothing will go wrong. Put yourself in the place of the English pigs. Why should they expect their boat to be hijacked at this time of the morning and here in Bridlington?' His dark face contorted with scorn. 'Knowing the English they'll be more concerned with getting yet another cup of that terrible tea they drink all the time, comrades.'

His words did the trick and Dick hissed, 'You can rely on us, comrade. We are young and inexperienced, but we shall carry out our sacred mission. Never fear.'

'Well said, comrade. Now here they come.' Inside his pocket the Palestinian clicked off the safety of his pistol in readiness.

'Char up, Flight,' the bespectacled little radio operator announced cheerfully as the grizzled flight sergeant in charge of the launch brought it to the mooring place.

'Ta, Johnson,' the grizzled NCO said, as the radio operator opened the big steel thermos and poured out a steaming mug of tea, 'I can use it. What bloody awful weather.' He stopped the engines and the sleek launch glided into the mooring.

On deck another RAF man, muffled in a thick raincoat, sprang onto the dock, with a mooring rope in his hands. Swiftly he tied the rope around the hawser.

Satisfied the NCO blew on his tea and took a sip. He could see from the clock above the launch's controls that they were only a couple of minutes later than usual. 'Made nice time though, Johnson, in spite of the weather.'

'Yer right, Flight. The paper shop up there'll be opening in half an hour. I'll nip up and get a couple of *Suns,* if that's all right with you, Flight?'

'All right with me, Johnson, as long as you don't take too long about it. Remember we *are* on duty.' He took another sip of his tea. 'See what kind o' tits the *Sun* is selling this morning. Cheer us up a bit before we have to go out in that sodding mess agen.' He indicated the snow which was falling in what appeared to be a solid white sheet. 'Christ, it's been snowing all bloody week now.' Automatically he turned on the radio to listen to the six o'clock news and the following shipping forecast.

Johnson poured himself a mug of tea. There was nothing to do in the radio room now and Flight was a nice old boy, with years of service behind him. Soon he was being posted to his last duty station in the Adriatic, 'to watch them bloody Yugs,' he meant Yugoslavs, 'bloody killing themselves.'

'It was announced yesterday,' the newsreader was saying, 'that the German Deutsche Bank will now run all its global operations from London. It is expected that the German Commerzbank, the other of the German big three high street banks, will follow suit shortly.'

Johnson sniffed, the steam from the tea rising up about his face. 'Looks as if the bloody Jerries are taking over, Flight,' he commented without any real malice as if it was simply a matter of fact.

'Ay,' the grizzled flight sergeant agreed. 'I was out there in Gütersloh at the time of the Gulf War and the sods wouldn't let us take our gear by rail to the port of embarkation. Lay down on the tracks they did, to stop us. Then they let us and the Yanks do their dirty washing for 'em. Now they're taking over–'

He stopped short suddenly. 'Hey,' he cried in alarm, lowering his mug to the little table, 'what's going on?'

The Palestinian raised his pistol, fitted now with the silencer. He knew instinctively that the grizzled middle-aged soldier, with the three stripes and a crown on his sleeve, was the boat's skipper and he needed him. So he fired at the one with spectacles.

Johnson yelped with pain as the slug slammed into his right shoulder. He dropped the mug and reeled against the bulkhead, blood spurting from the sudden wound in a scarlet arc.

'You bastard!' the flight sergeant yelled. He flung his mug at the Palestinian. The latter felt the scalding hot tea drench his face painfully. For a moment he lowered his guard. The old NCO didn't hesitate. He dived forward. The tackle caught the Palestinian around the waist. He went down. His finger tightened instinctively on his trigger. The pistol fired. A slug went through the bulkhead and then NCO was on top of him, smelling of male sweat and anger, punching and punching at his face.

His nose smashed. Warm blood streamed down into his open gasping mouth. He wriggled and writhed, trying to escape that deadly beating. But there was no escaping. The NCO held on to him, slamming his right fist into the Palestinian with dogged, angry relentlessness.

'Johnson, raise the frigging alarm!' he panted, as he continued to beat the intruder.

'Try yer best. Off yer go.'

'Sarge,' the other man gasped. Painfully he raised himself and staggered to the door of the bridge. He opened it. He caught a glimpse of other shadowy figures in the white gloom outside and realized instantly there were more of these strange intruders. His arm hurt like hell, but he reacted instantly. He ducked into the shadows. As noiselessly as he could, he started to make his way to the radio room.

On the little bridge, the Palestinian fought against fainting. As the NCO slammed yet another punch at his battered, bleeding face, he tried to stop the red mist of unconsciousness overcoming him. He had lost his pistol, but he still had his knife.

Desperately, knowing he would black out

soon, his fingers sought for it in his pocket. Then he had it. He seized the hilt eagerly, as the flight sergeant hit him yet again. But even now, when he was on the point of out, he remained rational. He knew they needed this man to steer the boat. He couldn't kill him, but he had to stop him punching him. He struck with the knife.

'*Ouch!*' the NCO yelped with pain, as the sharp blade ripped the length of the fingers of his right hand. 'You've bloody cut me!' he gasped and stopped hitting the intruder.

Groggily, the Palestinian reached out and found the pistol. Speaking through lips which felt puffy and awkward, he said, levelling it at the sergeant, who was hugging his wounded hand, 'That's enough of that. Get back to that wheel.' The Palestinian sat up, wondering if he would be able to get to his feet.

Eyes blazing furiously, the flight sergeant backed off, trailing blood behind him from his wounded hand. It was then that Dick came in. He saw the Palestinian squatting on the deck. He rushed to him. 'Comrade!' he exclaimed.

The Palestinian swallowed hard. Despite his injuries he felt a sense of love for the handsome young boy, who was obviously so concerned about him. 'I'll be all right. Just give me a hand to get to my feet.'

Tenderly Dick placed his arm about the Palestinian and drew him up. In that instant the Palestinian would have dearly loved to have kissed Dick on the lips. But he restrained himself. He said instead, 'Just keep an eye on that old pig, while I get my breath back.'

'I could kill him for what he's done to you,' Dick said fiercely, dark eyes blazing with anger.

The Palestinian shook his head and wished he hadn't. His face hurt like hell. 'No, we need him. Shout to Harry though, that the one I shot got away. We must stop him before he raises the alarm, *quick!*'

Dick opened the door to the bridge and shouted to Harry on the deck below.

Crouching in the shadows, feeling faint and weak, the blood still pouring from his wounded shoulder, Johnson couldn't understand the Arabic, but he guessed the shout had something to do with him. They were after him. He knew that by now they had bagged the two engine room artificers, plus old Flight. That left him alone. What the hell was he to do?

The klaxon! It came to him like a vision. If he could only get to the klaxon just in front of the bridge and sound the alarm, that would do it. There was always someone on duty in the harbour master's office on the jetty opposite the fish dock. They'd hear it and report to the authorities.

Johnson breathed out hard. Pink bubbles formed on his lips. That frightened the young bespectacled airman. Did that mean the bullet had penetrated to his lungs? He needed a doctor urgently. He pulled himself together. He had to reach that klaxon first. That was his duty. Dimly he could hear them shouting. They were after him, he was sure of that.

Crouching low he started to crawl across the freezing deck to the klaxon. Every few seconds, he could see the object clearly outlined in the revolving green light at the entrance to the harbour. It seemed so temptingly close, yet so far away.

Five feet to go. It felt like five miles to him. He was sobbing with pain now, his hands frozen and unfeeling.

As a kid he had loved those old forties movies about flying they had shown on late TV – *Reach for the Stars*, *The Dambusters* and the like, and those old-fashioned patriotic films had in a way inspired him to join the RAF even though he knew with his rotten eyes he could not aspire to becoming air crew.

But now, as he crawled on the frozen deck, he told himself that those romantic young men of half a century before, with their moustaches, cool, clipped manner and slang that no one understood any more – 'wizard prang', 'went for a Burton', and the like – would never have given up as he was tempted. Though wounded, they would have gone on till they died; 'pressing on regardless', as they would have called it. He must do the same.

He levered himself up and started crawling once more. He advanced at a pitiful rate of inches, his blood splashing on to the deck in great red gobs against the sparkling frosty surface. *'Do not despair for Johnny-head-in-the-air. He sleeps as sound as Johnny underground.'* The poem he remembered from that RAF movie with Michael Redgrave was going through his head now, as the red mist threatened to overcome him. *'Fetch out no shroud for Johnny-in-the-cloud. And keep your tears. For him in after years...'*

He was almost there now, gasping, as if he were running a great race.

He could hear the snarl and roar of the dogfight now. There it was – good old Spit, going after the Jerry Messerschmitt, fight Brownings spitting out tracer...

'There he is, the bastard.' George yelled. 'He's going to sound that siren. Get him – *quick!'*

Harry raised his pistol, hand trembling with excitement. He pressed the trigger. The slug howled off the bulkhead just above Johnson's head. Crazed with pain, but determined, he cried, 'Tallyho! Bandits at twelve o'clock high!' Next moment he pressed the klaxon's button and in the same instant that its shrill blast echoed and re-echoed across the little port, the second bullet shattered his spine.

Up on the little bridge, the Palestinian, not yet recovered from the beating he had taken, cried to Dick, 'Make the old bastard start her up at–'

Two beams of blinding white light came from both sides of the harbour, turning night into day, illuminating the whole of the launch. Dick shielded his eyes against the light and dug his pistol into the flight sergeant's side cruelly. 'Come on, start her up. I'll blow your guts out if you don't.'

'Go and fuck yersen!' the NCO retorted angrily.

Dick didn't hesitate. He slashed the muzzle of his pistol back and forth across the NCO's face. His nose snapped and a great gob of bright red blood dropped onto the, deck as he staggered backwards. 'Next time it'll be for keeps!' Dick yelled, feeling in complete charge of the situation.

'Quick ... quick!' the Palestinian urged, as the howl of a police siren started to come closer. 'They're on to us!'

'Well?' Dick demanded, thrusting the

pistol into the NCO's ribs.

'All right, bugger yer. But yer can't get away with this. This launch belongs to the Royal—'

'Move!'

Reluctantly the flight sergeant started the engine. He opened the throttles. Slowly the launch began to pull away from the quay. Behind them a police car skidded to a halt in the snow, as the two search lights followed their progress on their way to the exit from the harbour.

'Faster!' the Palestinian urged, as he spotted someone running swiftly along the wall to the exit. He knew that these days they had armed response squads in the British police. Was this an armed policeman?

Dick dug his pistol into the reluctant skipper's ribs once more. 'Make her go faster—'

The shot rang out. The glass in front of him shattered. It was an armed policeman.

On deck, Harry spotted the dark figure crouched there, both hands clasping a pistol. He sprang over Johnson's dead body, crouched and fired. The figure reeled back with a shrill cry. There was a splash as he fell into the water. Harry swung round and fired a second shot. The first of the two searchlights trained on the fleeing craft went out suddenly.

Then, as the flight sergeant pulled back the throttles, the launch's nose tilted upwards and she surged forward, throwing up a huge wake behind her. Minutes later she had disappeared into the morning. They were on the last stage of the last journey.

Chapter Two

'The balloon's gone up!' the Brig roared over the phone. 'Now it's shit or bust. Excuse the coarse expression, but that's the way we used to talk as young subalterns a long, long time ago.'

'Be my guest, sir,' Seal said happily with a grin. He could sense the Brig's excitement. All old soldiers were like that. They said in public they didn't like war or action, but they did. It was the shot in the arm they needed after the dull routine of barracks life.

As his old CO in the Royal Marines had always maintained, before he had trans-ferred to the SBS, 'War means promotion, old chap. Always remember that. Gongs and promotion.' There he had always grinned and added, 'If it don't, remember to make a pretty corpse.'

'What happened, sir?' Seal asked, looking

at the snow still flying in white fury outside.

'Fifteen minutes ago, they hijacked an RAF rescue launch.'

'Our people?'

'Very definitely. It's up to you now. The Harrie's standing by.'

'What about the rig, sir? Have they been alerted?'

'That's the bloody annoying part. We can't raise them. Perhaps their radio phone's out. Whatever it is, they don't know what's heading their way.'

Seal sniffed. 'How long do you think we've got before they hit the *Margaret Thatcher*, sir?' he asked.

'Matter of minutes. Bridlington to the rig, is at the most thirty minutes, even though the weather is exceedingly dirty at the moment.'

'Got to get my skates on, sir, then?'

'Exactly. Won't keep you any longer. Go to it, my boy. Good hunting.'

'Thank you, sir.'

The Brig put down the phone and turned to Daisy who was sitting opposite. She was pale and wore no make-up, but despite the early hour and the fact that he summoned her out of her bed, she was awake and for once not hung-over. When he had commented, she had replied, 'I think I might become a nun in the order of the fucked-up vestals.'

He had shaken his head sadly and said, 'Oh Daisy, my wonderful dear Daisy, don't talk in that cynical fashion. You've got so many years in front of you. Things can change.'

She had looked challengingly at him, cigarette crooked in the side of her broad expressive mouth, her eyes curled up against the smoke. 'Do you really think so, sir?'

'Of course. Why would I be spending my declining years in this damned business if I didn't think so?'

She held out both hands, palms outwards as if to ward him off. 'I know, sir, I know. But what does it all matter? We're such a pathetic little country now. When I studied German at university, I learned a phrase from an Austrian journalist – forget his name now. But the phrase lingers. "In the time of the setting sun, the dwarf appears to be a giant." Aren't our leaders, whatever party, like that today?'

But they don't count,' he said earnestly. 'Politicos and politicians are not what it's all about. One day – one day soon, God willing, power must come and be wielded like people such as we are. From the basis.'

She looked up at him, his face so earnest, so sad in a way because he still believed in something which was long dead, had been dead, these many years. 'But what can be done?' she asked.

'We've got to change before it's too late. England has got to be cleaned up. We can't just drift as we are doing now,' the Brigadier said, voice full of passion.

'We're just a little off-shore island, sir,' she said, feeling sorry for him. Did he really know what was going on out there in the mean streets?

'To be sure. But once that little island made a third of the world its own.'

'But it's such a long time ago.' She hesitated, then she said it, 'The spirit seems to have gone, sir, that's all.'

He looked at her shocked. *'Don't say that!'*

he said. 'That can't be true.'

She looked at the new snow drifting down sadly outside the window and nodded.

He shook his head proudly. 'I refuse to believe that,' he said, but the conviction had gone out of his voice.

Now the whole of Northern England was on red alert. At the Yorkshire airfields, Linton-on-Ouse and the rest, every available plane, even trainers were ready for action. Naval craft were heading for the East Coast at top speed. The 5th Rapid Response Brigade had been put on two hours' notice. Everywhere the authorities were preparing for the worse possible scenarios. Only on the *Margaret Thatcher* were they totally unaware of the danger coming their way, for the radio was still out.

As Baron von Klarsfeld told an emergency meeting of UK Oil's directors, some of them unshaven and one even in his bedroom slippers, for they had been dragged from their homes at top speed and brought to Central London in a fleet of hired cars, 'We all now know what's going to happen to the rig, and our chairman, *Major*,' he emphasized the rank with a sneer, 'Honor is on the *Margaret Thatcher* playing the role of a damned foreman.'

Someone objected, but the American moneyman, Trix from Houston, snorted, 'Herr von Klarsfeld's damn right. What in the damned Sam Hill is he doing up there, two hundred miles away when we've got this kind of crisis on our hands?' He bit on his cigar as if he might snap it in two. 'Now what are we going to do?'

There was silence for a few moments in the elegant boardroom, with reproduction Regency furniture and genuine oils on the walls. Hilary, at her little table to one side of the boardroom one, looked from one well-fed face to the next. She told herself that all they were concerned about was money and the power that money could buy. They weren't out in a rig in the middle of North Sea working twelve hour shifts in some of the worse weather for years.

Baron von Klarsfeld rose to his feet this time, as if rising would make what he had to say more significant. 'Gentlemen,' he said clearing his throat then rather pedantically. 'Nearly a century ago, during the Boxer Rebellion in China, the German Kaiser is reported to have said "the Chermans to ze front".' He gave a passable imitiation of someone imitating a German speaking poor English. One or two of his listeners laughed and he smiled at their response. 'Now I think it is time to repeat that statement. I suggest, gentlemen, that as I represent the largest investment in UK Oil, I should take over the temporary chairmanship of the company.' He beamed at them, obviously very pleased with himself.

There were a few shocked murmurs from the English members of the board and De Boers, the Dutchman, whose father had been in a German concentration camp, said sharply, 'I don't agree with that.'

But the Americans nodded their agreement and Trix said, 'I think that would be the best idea for the time being.'

'Thank you gentlemen,' von Klarsfeld said and added quickly, 'I suggest the following. We wait till the present crisis has been solved by the authorities. Then we make some decisions about UK Oil – and quick. We can't continue pumping money into a failing company. That is obvious. But for the time being, let us leave it at that.'

The members of the board started to get to their feet and Hilary said hastily, doing the same, 'There's coffee and tea and breakfast snacks in the ante-room.'

De Boers said thank you on their behalf but he didn't go into the ante-room. Instead he looked at von Klarsfeld angrily, muttered, *'eine verdammte Schweinerei,'* and stalked out.

Von Klarsfeld shrugged and strolled over to where Hilary stood. 'De Boers just said it was "a damned piggery" in German. Obviously the remark was aimed at me.' Again he shrugged carelessly. 'These small people like the Dutch have simply got to realize that they'll have to bow to our wishes these days, if we're ever going to do anything with Europe.'

'I seem to have heard that somewhere before, *Herr Baron.*' She emphasized the German title maliciously.

'Don't be silly thing, Hilary. Hitler was an

unfortunate hiccup in German history. We're not that kind of people really.' He smiled at her. 'I hope you'll have another think about the offer I made you the other day. It looks as if I shall be spending a lot of time in London now, doesn't it?'

She didn't answer his question. Instead she said, 'Is there no way that Major Honor can be warned?'

'I am sure your authorities are doing the best we can. But,' he lowered his voice and touched her hand, 'we must be prepared for the worse, you know.' With that he followed the rest into the ante-room.

She fought back her tears, tears of frustration, rage and sorrow. 'Let him be all right and safe,' she prayed fervently to herself. 'Let him win at last... Please God!'

On the rig, they were working flat out despite the weather, that was as bad as ever. The drilling operation was reaching its peak and they all knew it. Already the first dark grey traces on the drill indicated that they were reaching oil-bearing shale and the knowledge that they were going to do it at last, lent fresh enthusiasm and spirit to them. Even Hurst was working as if this was the start of the six day shift instead of nearly its end.

Honor watched them with pride, his own face unshaven and with dark circles of fatigue beneath his eyes. 'It's like in war, Red,' he cried above the noise and the howl of the wind. 'In war you know you just have to pull together as a team or you're for the chop.'

Red nodded sagely and answered, 'It *is* a war, Major. Only we're fighting a battle with nature. But now we're winning,' he added enthusiastically. 'We've got the old cow on the frigging run.'

The Major grinned wearily. 'You can say that again. And about bloody time too. Anyway, I'll just go over to the radio shack and see if Jacko has got the communications working again.' Body bent against the terrible wind which lashed the oilskin against his lean body, Major Honor fought his way into the radio shack.

Despite the cold there were beads of sweat on Jacko's face, as he worked on the radio from which came a crackle of static, morse and the occasional call in clear. 'How it's going, Jacko?' he asked.

'Well, something's working, sir. I can't send, but I do seem to be receiving.' He frowned. 'But there's something going on so everything is distorted.'

'What do you mean?' Major Honor asked, shaking the drops of moisture from his hard hat.

'Well, this time of the morning there's hardly any traffic normally. Today everybody and his bloody son seem to be on the air. Military and civvie. The airways are crowded to bursting.'

'Hmm,' Honor mused. 'That is strange. But keep trying to send. I want to signal UK Oil HQ that we seem to be hitting paydirt at long last–'

'Sir.' It was Red Ross standing in the door of the radio shack.

'What is it?'

'Something funny, sir. There's an RAF rescue launch approaching the rig. Just spotted her in a break in the snowstorm.'

Major Honor frowned. 'That's strange.

What do you think they want around here? Besides, they should know better than anyone, that's there's an exclusion zone around rigs, which must not be infringed.'

'Perhaps there's trouble, Major?'

'All right, let's have a look-see.'

Together they hurried outside and peered into the whirling storm in the direction indicated by Red Ross.

But the patrol boat seemed to have vanished. So after a few minutes of looking in vain, they gave up, with Major Honor saying, 'Perhaps they realized that they were off course when they saw the rig and moved on.'

Red Ross looked doubtful. 'Seems to me, sir, that they were heading towards us, as if they knew exactly where they were going.'

'Well, let's not worry about it,' the other man answered. 'Let's see what the latest is on the drill.'

The latest news was good. The sample cores coming up from deep below were getting darker and darker. Together they examined them, ignoring the storm raging all around them, as they stared at them in delight. 'It looks good, Red,' Honor said enthusiastically.

'You can say that again, sir,' the other man agreed. 'Another hour and then we'll have done it.'

'I think so, Red,' the Major agreed with a sudden note of relief in his voice. 'I smuggled a bottle of scotch aboard when I came. When we hit oil, damn company regulations about hard booze, we open that bottle and every man of the shift gets a drink.'

'With you, sir.'

But Major Honor was not fated ever to drink that smuggled scotch.

Chapter Three

The Cobra attack helicopters caught the terrorists by complete surprise as they fell out of the grey sky and came zooming in at wavetop height, churning the sea into a white fury below them. Harsh white beams of light encircled the launch and blinded the Palestinian up on the bridge watching the RAF NCO.

A voice boomed over a loud hailer, 'Stop that craft at once. Or there will be serious trouble.' Then the first helicopter had swept by them and commenced dancing above them, while the second one took up its position, missiles levelled at the little yellow launch menacingly.

Suddenly worried, the Palestinian stared up at the chopper circling above them. Vaguely he could see the white-helmeted pilot and another crew member strapped into the open hatch, holding on to a heavy machine gun.

Would they fire on their own people? he asked himself urgently. If they knew his mission, which he suspected they did, perhaps they would. The English, as decadent and soft as they were, had a ruthless streak, as did many weak people. He made his decision. 'George,' he yelled to the other terrorist on the deck below, as the launch started to slow down, 'get one of those two men from below. Show the bastards what we will do, if they don't leave us in peace.'

George needed no urging. Things were beginning to go wrong and the Palestinian, the expert who had been in this business for over twenty years, was the only one who knew how to get them out of trouble. He clattered down into the engine room.

Moments later he reappeared, leading in front of him a frightened artificer in overalls, prodding him in the back with his pistol.

The first helicopter circled once more, illuminating the deck with that harsh white light. The Palestinian leaned out of the bridge and yelled above the roar of the chopper, 'Force him on his knees. Say you will kill him if they don't go away. *Quick!*'

George forced the terrified RAF man down on his knees on the swaying deck, as the chopper danced in the air above them. That tremendous metallic voice cried, 'Now stop this tomfoolery at once. Just give up and let's call it a day—'

The voice stopped suddenly. George had placed his pistol muzzle against his captive's left temple. It was obvious what the terrorist intended to do.

The Palestinian could sense the pilot's hesitancy. He waved his hand and indicated that the pilot should leave. He watched as the latter spoke urgently into his mike. The Palestinian guessed he was asking for orders. Moments later he knew he had been right, for the two helicopters turned and began to fly away, disappearing into the fresh snowstorm. He breathed a sigh of relief. They had pulled it off. Now nothing could stop them.

Chapter Four

'Joyfuckingriders!' Sergeant Hargreaves said bitterly, pronouncing the term as one word. 'I'd give 'em fucking joy riding!'

Despite the tension, Seal smiled. Hargreaves had just heard over the phone from his wife in Poole, that some kid had stolen the family car overnight and, having wrecked it, had run off. It was something that happened all the time elsewhere, but not usually in Poole, to members of the Special Boat Service. The kids there knew better.

'I blame the bleeding parents. They don't know how to bring up their sodding kids – scared of them,' Hargreaves ranted on. 'Then at school there's no discipline, not even a cane to larrup the little buggers with. Those poofter parlour pinks saw to that in the Seventies. Even the coppers can't give 'em a clip around the ear like they used to do in the old days, when I was a kid.' By now Hargreaves' hard face was almost purple with rage. 'Then in the end they go and feather-bed the sods so that they don't know how to fend for themselves, and start producing more little bastards like themselves on the welfare state. *Joy frigging riding!* There'd be no frigging joy to it if I had my way,' he ended darkly.

Seal was amused but at the same time troubled. He had heard that kind of talk in bars and clubs all over the country, not from the rich and privileged, but from ordinary working people like Hargreaves. It was all part and parcel of the general malaise that the Brig was intending to fight. People were sick of the scroungers and petty crooks, who recognized no authority and no law. 'They will ruin this nation completely,' the Brig was wont to say, 'if something drastic is not done soon.'

'Sir,' the respectful voice cut into his reverie.

He turned sharply and Hargreaves stopped ranting, immediately the calm, collected trained professional.

The messenger wore the uniform of the RAF, and he looked a little flustered, as if he had a lot on his mind and wanted to get rid of it swiftly.

Seal nodded. 'Morning, Corporal. What is it?'

'The squadron commander says we're in business. They've spotted the hijacked Air Sea Rescue launch with the wanted men on board, heading for the rig.'

Seal whistled softly. This was it, though he didn't like the thought of what was to come.

'The terrorists made the chopper boys back off and now the squadron commander says it'll have to be up to you. He's whistled up a Harrier with pods. It's just landed and I'm to take you there at double quick time, sir. Everything's ready for you – weapons, stun grenades, the works.'

Seal sprang to his feet. He nodded to the rest of the Alpha Team. That sufficed. Nothing more needed to be said.

Ten minutes later they were standing in ankle-deep snow on the football field of some Hull manufacturing company, waiting for the Harrier to come down. In the meantime the squadron leader, a brisk young man who wore the Gulf Medal, briefed them. 'The chopper boys spotted four of them before they were driven off by one of them threatening to shoot one of our bods. They tried to keep up with them, but there was a sudden white-out and they lost them, but it was perfectly obvious that they were heading for the *Margaret Thatcher*.'

'Has the rig crew been informed?' Seal asked.

'No, that's the damn frustrating thing about this all. We can't raise the rig. Something must have gone wrong with their radio – or it's been sabotaged or something.' The squadron leader looked very worried.

Seal opened his mouth to say something, but the whine of jet engines made him pause. He looked up, as did the others. It was the Harrier with what looked like two camouflaged fuel tanks beneath its stubby wings.

Hurriedly the squadron leader shouted above the noise as the Harrier started to descend vertically. 'I don't need to tell you chaps the drill.'

'No you don't, I suppose,' Seal answered a little dolefully, as the Harrier landed in a flurry of snow and they could see the pods more clearly. 'Damn things!'

'I know what you mean,' the squadron leader agreed, 'but then orders is orders.' He held out his hand. 'Best of luck, old chap.'

'Thank you.' Seal turned to Hargreaves after shaking the RAF officer's hand. 'All right you take the port pod with your chap. I'll take starboard with Dusty Rhodes here.'

'Rightho, sir.' Together Hargreaves and the other marine ploughed through the ankle-deep snow to the far pod and opened the hatch cover. Seal watched for a moment, while the two men arranged themselves with their weapons and equipment in the pod, and then attached their earphones which linked them with the pilot. An RAF mechanic closed the hatch and Hargreaves waved through the little porthole, though Seal knew he felt like he did about the pods. 'Like being in a metal coffin,' he had commented more than once.

Five minutes later Seal and Rhodes were locked inside their pod, with Seal linked to the pilot by the headphones. Since they had last been carried in the pods, new technology had reduced the noise and the vibration as the Harrier took off. Still as the jet started to climb into the grey, snow-filled sky, Seal wasn't too happy. He tried to dismiss his apprehension as he called his instructions to the unseen pilot, ending with, 'Get rid of us quick, then beat it. We'll do the rest.'

'Right,' the pilot's voice came cheerfully over the intercom. 'Rather you than me, old mate.' Then they were flying the length of the snowbound Humber, heading for the North Sea – and action.

Now excitement was growing by the minute on the *Margaret Thatcher*. The cores dug from the sea bottom were getting darker and darker and everyone was bracing himself automatically for the first thrilling gush of oil, which would erupt from the sea around the rig. Time and time again men working on the platform would hurry to peer over the side at the sea, many hundred feet below.

Even the cooks, a notoriously miserable breed, always offended because no one ever seemed to like their food, were happy this day as they came with tea and sandwiches at regular intervals. 'Bacon butties or steak sandwiches at ten?' they chortled as they, too, stared at the green pounding sea. '*Yorkshire Relish* and all for anybody that wants it.'

In the excitement the spotting of the Air Sea Rescue launch had been forgotten. Today they wanted to strike oil, for tomorrow their shift would be ending and all of them, including Hurst, wanted to be able to tell their mates in Hull, who were in the same industry, that 'we've done it. *We've struck oil!*'

By now they were drilling in a high pressure zone, exerting upwards at a pressure of 9,000 pounds a square inch. It was an awesome pressure which would destroy everything on the rig, if they lost control. But Red Ross was keeping the stuff down with a mixture of chemicals circulating in the mud pumps. But it needed careful monitoring. Every five minutes or so he stepped over to the gauge to check on the mud balance.

It was there that Jacko caught him, as he was checking the density of the mud holding the high pressure in place. 'Red ... Red!' the radio operator cried above the hum of the machinery and the howl of the storm, his face frantic.

Red Ross held up his hand as he peered at the gauge. 'Hold it ... hold it for half a mo,' he commanded, while Jacko almost stamped his feet with suppressed excitement and fear.

Finally he looked up and saw the look on the little radio operator's face. 'What's up, Jacko?' he asked baldly.

'The radio's started working again. I'm getting incoming and outcoming.'

'And?'

'So, I've just had a warning.'

'What?'

'An emergency. A group of terrorists have hijacked an RAF launch at Brid, and are heading this way. Red, we're in real trouble, I tell you...'

'Jesus Christ, not that, too!' Red groaned.

Then he remembered the yellow-painted launch he had glimpsed briefly, some minutes before through the storm. Was that the hijacked launch? He made a swift decision. 'All right, Jacko, back to the shack at the double and keep listening. I'm going to tell the Major.'

Jacko fled.

With George digging the muzzle of his pistol into the NCO's ribs, the grizzled RAF man steered the launch carefully to the side of the rig which towered above them. On the deck the Palestinian and Dick tensed, as the launch bobbed up and down in the heavy swell, trying to judge the right moment to launch themselves into space. It was going to be tricky, but the Palestinian was convinced Dick was young and fit enough to do it. He, himself had, been training for this part of the operation for three months. He knew *he* could do it. He raised his voice. 'All right, Dick, I'm counting to three, then I'm off. You follow.'

The other man nodded his understanding. The Palestinian began to count. *'Three!'*

He jumped. He slammed into a stanchion. His hands which he had dusted with French chalk, especially for the long climb, caught on the wet metal and held. For a moment he hung on there, gasping a little. Then he turned and faced Dick, balancing on the prow which bobbed up and down and commanded, as he extended one hand, 'Now!'

'Yes Comrade.' Dick sprang from the launch. His foot slipped and he began to cry out, but the Palestinian caught him in time before he went under. Exerting all his strength, he tugged upwards. For a moment or two they just hung there, regaining their strength while on the bridge of the launch George held up one arm in triumph, like a boxer who has just knocked out a tough opponent.

Finally the Palestinian was ready. 'It looks tough, but it isn't really. There are rails for support on both sides of the ladder. All it takes is stamina. Come on, let's go.' He reached up to the first wet dripping rung of the steel ladder which led upwards and began the ascent. Behind, a little more apprehensively though, Dick started to do the same. Behind them George forced the grizzled NCO to moor the launch close to the base of the rig, so that from above it would be difficult to see. Then he stared upwards as his two comrades continued their long and arduous ascent. Metre by metre they toiled upwards towards the platform...

On the platform, a worried Red Ross talked about the new situation to an equally worried Major Honor.

'We've got a couple of shotguns, that's all the police will authorize us to have,' Red said.

'I've got a pistol. We're outside the twelve mile limit, Red, so the police can't really tell us what we can do.' Major Honor sniffed. 'But a couple of twelve-bores and a pistol aren't much use against terrorists, I suppose.' He walked to the side of the platform and peered into the white gloom. 'No further sign of that missing RAF launch,' he said. 'Surely,' he added, as if to reassure himself, 'our people will be here before them. The Navy and RAF must have been alerted by now.'

'Yes, I suppose so, Major,' Red Ross agreed but there wasn't much conviction in his voice. He couldn't see how helicopters would be able to land in weather like this. It would be up to the Navy and it'd be one hell of a climb from the sea to the platform. 'We'll just have to play it by ear,' he concluded in the end.

Major Honor nodded his agreement and together they drifted back to the mud gauge and began checking progress once more.

The climb was harder than the Palestinian had bargained. In the training he had undergone on Iraqi rigs in the Gulf, he had not had to contend with such terrible weather, simply with the climb itself. Here the wind and bitter squalls of snow, whipped against their faces and bodies every few seconds, and threatened to rip them from their precarious perches at any moment.

Once Dick almost slipped and screamed. But the Palestinian didn't hear in the howling wind and, after he had steadied himself, Dick continued to follow him up.

The sea cheated of its prey fell back with a angry hiss.

Now, gasping like ancient asthmatics in the throes of an attack, they could see the platform and their nostrils were now assailed by the stink of diesel. At that moment it smelled better than any perfume of any woman Dick had bedded.

They were almost there. The deck was just above them.

Five minutes later, shaking all over with the strain, soaked and worn, they hauled themselves over the side of the steel platform and collapsed behind a pile of rusting oil drums in the mud. *They had done it!*

How long they lay there, the Palestinian didn't know, but slowly as the feeling started to come back into his hands, he unzipped his soaked wind breaker and took out the little Uzi sub-machine-gun. A moment later Dick did the same. Cautiously they raised themselves from their hiding place and stared at the busy scene in front of them: men operating machinery, others lugging pipes back and forth, while others stared at the whirling drill, as if it were very fragile and needed constant attention.

'There's the radio shack,' the Palestinian hissed. 'That's your job, Dick.'

'Understood, comrade.'

'I shall tackle the crew. But let us wait five minutes and see that they are all there. After all there are two of us and at least twelve or more of them.'

In silence they studied the men working on the platform and in the end the Palestinian concluded that they were all present, including the two cooks, who had just brought up a tray of steaming sandwiches and a thermos from the galley below. He nodded to Dick. 'Off you go. You have got the message?'

'Yes comrade.'

'Move!'

Dick needed no urging. Ducked low, he headed for the radio shack, with its bright gleaming aerial and radar dome, Uzi tucked into his hand. The Palestinian nodded his approval and then he moved carefully, climbing on to a little derrick above the main platform, still unseen by the busy workers. He levered himself up behind some

286

drums of oil that lay there and, pulling out his grenades, placed them carefully on the top of one of the drums. He took in the scene for one last time, then he acted. The first grenade hissed through the air.

It exploded with a flash of savage, violet light. Shrapnel hissed through the air. Hurst was hit. He clawed the air in his unbearable agony, as if he were climbing the rungs of an invisible ladder. A second later he went over the side of the platform to plunge to his death four hundred feet below.

Aghast the suddenly white-faced workers turned to stare in the direction from which the grenade had come. They saw the Palestinian crouched there, little Uzi at the ready. Red Ross yelled something angrily. The Palestinian ignored the shout. Instead he jerked up the muzzle of the little sub-machine-gun menacingly and cried, 'Hands up the lot of you – *quick!*'

Slowly, reluctantly, they began to raise their hands, all save one of them, Major Honor. He had just returned from the heads and was still hidden by the oil drums, parked on both sides of the roped-off space which led to the heads. He ducked instinctively, telling himself it had happened. They, the terrorists, had taken over already, What the hell was he going to do?

Chapter Five

The radio message caused consternation among some of the directors of UK Oil, for they knew this had to be the end for their hopes in the North Sea.

It read: 'To the reactionary government of England. We have taken the *Margaret Thatcher* rig with nearly twenty prisoners. They shall come to no harm if our conditions are met. These are (1) This message is to be published on the front pages of the *Times*, the *Telegraph* and the *Independent*. (2) The Prime Minister of England shall make a public apology for unleashing the criminal war on Iraq in 1990. (3) That we will be allowed to leave the Rig unharmed when we have completed our task here. Finally, if the English Prime Minister does not make his apology to Iraq at prime minister's question time at three o'clock this afternoon, we shall begin killing the hostages one by one.'

'No prime minister would agree to that,' someone said, 'especially with the elections coming up soon.'

'Perhaps he could stall till the Armed Forces arrive,' someone else suggested.

'Doubt it,' von Klarsfeld said easily. 'As soon as the soldiers appear, these people will start shooting the hostages. These terrorists have nothing to lose in a situation like that and everything to gain. Oh yes, they'll shoot them all right, you can be sure.' He looked at his polished, well-manicured nails, as if he were well pleased with his own sagacity.

'Well, what do you suggest?' someone around the board table asked.

'Go ahead with their demands. Put their statement in the papers mentioned and then see what happens.' Von Klarsfeld's voice hardened. 'What ever happens, one thing is definitely clear.'

'What's that, Klarsfeld?' Twix, the American banker from Houston, asked, although he already knew the answer.

'UK Oil is bankrupt. Those of us who still have confidence in the operation, will have to start looking around for fresh backers as soon as the company is wound up. I think, with a bit of luck, I can find those backers.' Again von Klarsfeld looked very pleased with himself.

'Yes,' de Boers, the Dutchman, said bitterly. 'In Frankfurt no doubt.'

Von Klarsfeld did not deign to answer, but Twix, who had been discussing the matter with the German most of the morning, said with enthusiasm, 'I think that would be the answer. The company re-formed with German backers would be a much more efficient organization.' He beamed, showing off his thick capped teeth and said in atrocious German, 'Vorsprung durch Technik, eh Klarsfeld?'

'Something like that.'

De Boers flushed red but said nothing, as did the other British members of the board. Von Klarsfeld looked around for a moment in his most democratic manner, waiting for any other comment. None came, so he said,

'Then I can declare this emergency meeting closed.' He rose to his feet. The others did the same. Twix winked at him knowingly. 'Hilary,' von Klarsfeld said, 'Have a moment?'

She came across. 'Sir?'

'Would you be kind enough as to contact the Cabinet Office and inform the people there, that we urgently request the PM to do as the terrorists demand.' He said the words without energy and she knew instinctively that he was saying them as a matter of form.

'But what about the men – Red Ross ... Major Honor?' she stuttered, very close to tears now. 'You can't let them die just like that, sir.'

'But that is not my problem, Hilary. That is a problem for your armed forces,' he replied blandly, totally unmoved by her appeal. 'Your soldiers are used to this sort of thing. They'll just have to try.'

'Can't you buy them off – the terrorists, I mean?' she said passionately. 'I've heard you say before, that anyone and anything can be bought, if you've got the money.'

He shook his head and placed his hand

soothingly on hers, 'Now calm down, my dear. You don't want to make a scene, you're English. No, these men are fanatics. One can't buy that type off.' He pressed her hand softly. 'It'll be over in the next twenty-four hours and soon it will be all forgotten – another nine day wonder. Then,' he looked swiftly to left and right to check if there was anyone listening to him, 'I shall make you happy, my dear.'

'Damn you!' she cried. Suddenly she wrenched her hand from his and did something that had never happened to Baron von Klarsfeld in all his well-ordered, protected life – she slapped him across the face – very hard.

'Why ... why did you do that?' he stuttered in shock.

'You wouldn't know, would you?' she answered, her eyes blazing now. 'All you know is your money and your power. Well, what's that based on, eh? I'll tell you. It's based on the efforts of those brave men out on the rig – and you're not prepared to lift a damn little finger.' She pushed him to one side. 'Oh, get out my way. I can't stand the sight of you a minute longer. You'll have my resignation in the post by ten o'clock.' With that she stalked off, leaving him to stare at her shapely back in total bewilderment...

'Listen,' the Harrier pilot said, 'the Prime Minister – yes, I did say the Prime Minister – has just been on the blower. He says we're engaged on a mission of national importance. He says, too, that we've got to deal with the terrorists on board the *Margaret Thatcher* by fourteen hours at the latest because at fifteen hundred he has to reply to an ultimatum they have set him in the House of Commons. In other words, old boy, this is all top level stuff. Clear?'

'Clear,' Seal, crouched in the long narrow tube, replied, wishing all this was over. Action was better than being cooped up like this under a plane, cutting through the snow storm at 500 mph. 'What's the drill?'

'Since the terrorists radioed their ultimatum, the rig's radio has gone as dead as a dodo, despite all attempts to raise the *Margaret Thatcher. So* we can assume that the terrorists are in full control there. Now my intention is to land for the briefest of intervals on the helipad above the main platform. With this hell of a storm and a bit of luck, I might be able to get down and be gone before they can react. Then, old boy, it's all yours and remember the eyes of the nation are upon you.' He chuckled.

Seal grinned. The pilot was a bit of a card. Still he was playing it cool. It was the right thing to do in these sorts of tense situation. 'How much more flying time?'

'At the most a couple of minutes. I've not spotted the rig–' He stopped short. 'Yes, there she is – about a thousand feet below. I can barely see her in the storm, which is all to the good, though it's going to be tricky trying to get onto the helipad. All right, here we go.' The intercom went dead.

Like a stone, making Seal's stomach churn unpleasantly, the Harrier dropped out the sky. There was a hefty thud and the stink of burning rubber, and then the pilot was crying, *'Out! One of them has spotted us!'*

Seal flung open the catches. Together with Rhodes he sprang out of the container. On the port side the other two SBS men did the same. The pilot waited no longer. Already Dick was raking the side of the plane with bullets. His engines roared. He started to rise. Then tragedy struck.

There was the stink of kerosene. Seal and the others crouched low, watched in horror as sudden flames started to lick the length of the vertical take-off plane. Desperately the pilot tried to keep the Harrier flying. To no avail! Abruptly it went out of control altogether. It dropped over the side of the rig, trailing flame behind it. A moment later they heard a tremendous splash followed an instant afterwards by the hiss of water striking flames.

'Poor sod,' Hargreaves said, and then they forgot the dead pilot as the bullets began to howl off the structure above them. 'Take cover,' Seal yelled. 'Return fire!'

'Look out!' Hargreaves shouted in alarm, but was whirled right round by the impact of a slug at such close range. It was the third terrorist, Harry, who had come up the little ladder leading to the helipad from behind, and surprised them. 'Bugger it,' Hargreaves said, as if surprised, then pitched face downwards onto the pad.

Rhodes let off a burst.

Harry was quicker. He ducked. The slugs ran the length of the steel deck where he had just been, raising a line of angry blue-red sparks.

'Christ!' Seal yelled. He tugged out a stunbomb, armed it in the same instant and lobbed it towards where the terrorist was hiding. A sharp crack. A scream and Harry went reeling, head over heel down the ladder. Seal rose to his feet. 'Down that ladder. Check Hargreaves, Rhodes.'

As they ran for the ladder and out of the fire coming from below, Rhodes paused for an instant at the still body of the NCO. He felt for a pulse. There wasn't one. 'Bought the farm, he has sir,' he yelled over the vicious snap-and-crackle of the fire fight.

Seal cursed. Together the three survivors went clattering down the ladder, out of sight of the Palestinian and Dick, who kept blasting the helipad with short bursts from the UZIs...

Major Honor, the only one of the rig's crew

who had not been shepherded into the messhall and locked in, knew that the help was on hand. He knew, too, that the terrorists had already prepared the rig for destruction. He had watched them carrying piles of gelatine dynamite cartridges down below the main platform and packing them against one of the metal legs. He didn't need a crystal ball to realize that once their job was done here, they'd clamber down to the hijacked RAF rescue launch below and be off, leaving the *Margaret Thatcher* to its fate. That was something he had to prevent. But how?

Then it came to Honor. Back on that ridge when the Chinese had come storming their positions, whistles shrilling, bugles blowing, in their thousands, they had run out of grenades. And it had been grenades thrown over the parapet down the stony hillside, which had broken up attack after attack. 'Windy' Williams, known as 'Windy' because he was the bravest man in the company, had solved the problem. 'Bottles,' he had yelled urgently, 'bottles and petrol, lads. We're going to make a few cocktails for our little yellow friends.'

They had stared at the big captain, as if he had gone off his head with the strain – 'bomb happy', as they called it. But he had smiled in return, as the Chinese down below had massed for yet another attack. *'Molotov cocktails,'* he had explained. 'A fire bomb.'

Now Major Honor remembered how they had taken the last jerricans of petrol – all their carriers had been knocked out so they no longer needed fuel – and collected any bottle they could find, empty Vat 69s, Bass Best Bitter and the like – and filled them with the highly flammable mixture. When the Chinese had come in yet another mass rush, screaming, shouting, as if they were high on drugs or drink, or perhaps both, they had been met by a flaming wall of fire. They had survived yet another day.

Now Major Honor started his preparations. He crept to the nearest petrol locker. The well-oiled key turned in the door noiselessly. There he found rows of jerricans of petrol, kept under lock and key for security purposes.

But where was a bottle? He remembered Jacko's habit of stashing a bottle away so that the rest of the crew wouldn't find it. He prayed that this might be Jacko's hiding place. He was lucky.

There was a half empty bottle of vodka hidden behind the second row of jerricans. He seized it eagerly, took a slug of the fiery spirit for courage and emptied out the rest.

Now, spilling quite a lot of the petrol, in his haste and nervousness, he filled it the best he could. When it was three-quarters full, he put the jerrican down, and crawled through the mud to the little shed where the gelatine dynamite was stored.

Gingerly he broke open one of the cartridges. One wrong move now and the whole lot might go up. Now he started forcing some of the gelatine into the bottle. It was a messy business and he had to keep wiping his fingers all the time, but slowly he began to fill the rest of the space in the bottle with the highly dangerous stuff.

Outside the sound of the fire-fight had died away. He wondered why. Had the terrorists retreated down to the spud, and were now preparing to blow their charges, which would bring the whole rig tumbling down? Or had they defeated the sudden intruders from the sky? He told himself not to bother about things he could do little about and get on with the job at hand.

Now the 'cocktail' was ready. Old Windy's cocktail of so long ago, when the nation and its fighting men had still believed – and *died* – because of that old patriotic England – in a remote foreign land which meant nothing to them. He ripped off his tie. He used all his strength to tear it in two. He forced one end into the neck of the bottle and somehow managed to screw the cap back on, leaving a bit of cloth hanging out. His fuse and 'cocktail' were ready.

He left the cover of the shed. He was going back to war.

Day Six

Saturday

'It was no picnic, despite what anyone might say later. Most of us were pretty scared all the bloody time; you only felt happy when the battle was over and you were on your way home. Then you were safe for a bit, anyway.'

Colin Gray, Battle of Britain pilot,
Winter 1940

Chapter One

'So the PM didn't make the statement, nor have the papers printed their statement,' Daisy said, puffing at her cigarette. Outside London was shrouded in fog and the sound of the capital's traffic was muted and remote.

'No,' the Brig answered, 'he told the Commons what had happened, said he wouldn't give in to terrorist blackmail and then promised retaliation if anything happened to the rig and the men on it.' The Brig laughed cynically. *'Retaliation'*. Remember how long it took us to get a force together for the Gulf five years ago? We were scraping the barrel then. Every second heavy tank we had in Germany for the op was a non-runner. No,' he sighed, 'it's just the same old parliamentary bluster. Anyway, as you know, the elections are coming up soon. It wouldn't do his party's chances much good then if he were seen giving into that bunch.'

Daisy drew on her cigarette, eyes wrinkled with the smoke and thought the Brig was beginning to look his age. Aloud she said, 'What's the latest, sir?'

'We simply don't know. The fog's closed in the whole of the North Sea and we haven't had a sighting of the rig since yesterday lunchtime. Nor has the Harrier taking in the SBS team returned to base.'

'What about radio contact, sir?'

'Now that's the funniest bit of them all. After the ultimatum was not accorded to by the PM at three o'clock yesterday afternoon, one would have thought that the terrorists would have started cracking the whip, making more threats over the radio. But there's been not a sausage from them since then.' He looked puzzled and worried.

Daisy stubbed out her cigarette. 'Could it be, sir,' she said sharply, 'that the terrorists' plans have gone wrong. Yesterday they held the whip hand over us, with the rig and the hostages, so why haven't they done something? Could something – someone – have

306

got in their way?'

Fresh hope crossed the Brigadier's face. 'By George, you might just well be right, Daisy!'

She lit another cigarette, face hard and tough. 'I'd just like to see those treacherous murderous bastards with their balls in a wringer, sir.'

'Language, Daisy!'

She didn't seem to hear. 'Christ, what I just wouldn't give to take the pigs out personally,' she snarled. 'They and their kind have been making our lives a misery now for – oh – these forty years, ever since Suez. It's about time it all came to an end and they went back to their frigging camels and tents.'

The Brigadier nodded his silent agreement, though his mind was elsewhere, wondering what was going on on the rig...

In the UK Oil boardroom, there were others who were wondering the same at that very moment. De Boers had called an early morning meeting of those who wanted to see UK Oil remain as it was. In addition to the Dutchman, there were the three British directors and Ferguson, the Canadian, plus Hilary Stevens, for von Klarsfeld had refused to accept her resignation even after being slapped by her.

He had said very grandly when she had presented it to him, 'It's no use, Miss Stevens, I refuse to accept your notice. You are too valuable to the company in this moment of crisis. You know everything. You will work out the terms of your contract and then you can go.' With that he had dismissed her and she had stumbled out of his office somewhat crestfallen.

Now she sat in her usual place to the side of the great boardroom table, notepad in her hand, waiting to take down anything of importance, as De Boers opened the meeting. 'Gentlemen,' he said, *'they,'* – they all knew who he meant by 'they' –'know there's oil down there and *we* do too. They are trying to freeze us out with the threat of bankruptcy. If we let them, then we will no longer be on this board in the New Year. They will relinquish us and then you'll know who will be running UK Oil.' He looked around their worried faces sternly.

One or two of them nodded their agreement, but none of them said anything.

'We can't let that happen,' De Boers said firmly. 'Somehow or other we must find more capital, even if it's only for a further week to keep the firm going.'

'May I say something?' a polite transatlantic voice enquired. It was Ferguson, the Canadian.

De Boers nodded, but said nothing.

Ferguson's craggy face, under the mop of bright red hair, grinned. 'Perhaps it's known to you, gentlemen, there is another "they" as far as we Canadians are concerned – the *Americans.*'

Hilary looked up. This sounds interesting, she told herself.

Ferguson continued, 'Last night I was onto certain people in Toronto. They are prepared to take a certain financial gamble.'

Every head suddenly swung in Ferguson's direction. The Canadian's bright eyes twinkled. 'Perhaps it'll be only a month's money, but UK Oil can have it.'

There were cries of 'bravo', and De Boers

exclaimed in Dutch, *'Gottverdamme.'*

'Yes.' Ferguson's twinkle vanished. 'But my principals insist on knowing what's going on on the *Margaret Thatcher* within twenty-four hours. They know full well that if it comes out that Canada is going to put up the capital, *they,*' he, too, emphasized the word carefully, 'will put on the pressure to close down the company. *Immediately!'*

'Then they shall not find out, gentlemen,' De Boers said fiercely, eyes blazing. 'It can't be long before we find out what is happening.' He threw a glance at the grey shrouded window, 'if only this damned fog would lift so that our planes can find out what is going on out there...'

Chapter Two

Major Honor was only too glad that the fog
was so thick. As he prowled the rig, home-
made fire bomb in his hand, stepping over
obstacles carefully, trying to make as little
noise as possible, he knew that the terrorists
had failed in part.

Up above he had heard how yesterday the
intruders from the sky had bottled up the
radio shack so that no message could be
sent or received (in fact what he didn't
know was that Dick had fired a burst into
the radios with his Uzi before fleeing with
the Palestinian). Honor had also heard how
one of the intruders from the sky had
ordered the shift to remain in their messhall
prison. It was safer there. Thereafter
nothing much happened, any sound muted
by the heavy fog, and he had guessed both
sides, the terrorists and the intruders, had
decided it was too dangerous to continue

operations at night and would wait for light to come.

Now it was light enough and Major Honor knew before the action started again he had to do something about those explosives packed to the side of the rig, which if exploded, would cause it to smash into the sea far below. He guessed the intruders, whoever they were, would know nothing of the demolition charges. Their first objective would be to take out the terrorists and then secure the rig. But then it would be too late.

The terrorists would set the timer and head back for the launch moored somewhere far below; and he knew that it was there, for twice during the freezingly cold night he had heard the launch's motors being started up, as if the terrorist in charge wanted to ensure that they would be ready when the time came.

Gingerly, very gingerly, wishing he was in his nice warm flat having his morning cup of tea, Major Honor put his foot on the first rung of the ladder which led to the explosives below. It was going to be tricky on the slippery steel ladder in the half-gloom, with the terrorists on the lookout for the first sign of trouble, but he knew he had to do it ...

Fifty feet above him on the platform, Seal nudged Corporal Rhodes in the ribs. 'All right, Dusty, I think we'd better move out and find 'em.'

'Can I request a quick transfer to the Army Pay Corps?' Rhodes whispered.

Seal grinned although he was chilled to the bone and stiff from crouching, curled up on the muddy steel platform all night, waiting for this dawn. 'I'll personally take care of it when we get back to base, Dusty. Come on.'

Rhodes' grin vanished and he cocked his little automatic carefully. There were hundreds of hiding places in the huge rig from which the terrorists could bushwhack them. They had to be on their toes for this one. From the messhall where the workers were still congregated, there came the sizzle and crackle of frying bacon. 'Lucky sods,' Rhodes said enviously as they approached the edge of the big platform and peered downwards, trying to pierce the white gloom.

Seal reasoned that the terrorists would be below the platform. They wouldn't want to cut off the escape route to the hijacked launch by being above the platform. Besides, the third man of the Alpha Team was stationed up there just for that eventuality. 'Dusty,' he said, 'I think we'll split up, once we're on the next level below. You to the right. I'll take the left quarter. Less of a target that way.'

'Yes Boss,' Rhodes agreed.

In silence they clambered down to the next stage, using the stanchions and not the ladder. On the ladder they would have been too obvious, an easy target. Again they paused, crouched low, all senses alert for anything unusual. There was nothing but the muted growl and hiss of the sea far below.

With a movement of his hand, Seal indicated that Dusty should continue. The latter nodded slowly to indicate he had understood. Like a grey ghost in the night, he vanished over the side down the stanchions to the next stage of their descent, while Seal covered him for a few moments, head tilted to one side, listening for the slightest suspicious noise...

The Palestinian put his mouth close to Dick's ear. 'They come!' he hissed urgently.

For a moment he could sense the boy's fear, then the latter got a grip on himself and nodded. He raised his Uzi. The Palestinian shook his head. Instead he drew the knife, with which he had killed the watchman at Skipsea, from his jacket. 'Too noisy,' he whispered into Dick's ear, fighting off the unreasoning urge in such a tight tense situation to kiss the boy.

The soft footsteps came closer and closer. The two men, waiting for the intruder, dare hardly breathe. Despite the freezing cold, the Palestinian felt the hand holding the knife was suddenly warm and wet with sweat.

A dark shape appeared some two or three metres away and paused as if the intruder was aware danger lay ahead for him. Silhouetted a stark black against the rolling grey of the fog, they could see the pistol held in his hand. He seemed to stay there for an age. Had he seen them, the Palestinian wondered in sudden alarm. But why didn't he shoot?

Then the figure moved again. It was coming down the rest of the ladder. The Palestinian felt the nerve twitching at the left side of his face. Tension mounted frighteningly. Now he could smell the intruder, a combination of male sweat, salt water and diesel oil. Now he was only half a metre away. In an instant he'd see them crouched there next to the stanchion. The time had come to act. He lunged forward with his deadly blade. The point hit something metallic and glanced to the right.

Dusty Rhodes fired instinctively. But his aim was wild, as he was caught off balance. His slugs howled off the steel girders all about. 'Bastard!' he cursed and lifted his pistol to take aim. The Palestinian didn't give him a second chance. His knife sunk deep into the pit of the SBS man's stomach. The Palestinian pulled it out instantly with an obscene sucking noise. He could feel his fingers suddenly wet with hot blood. He lunged again.

Dusty Rhodes' spine arched like the taut string of a bow. A terrible strangled cry came from his gaping mouth, as he tried to keep his balance. To no avail. Frantically his fingers fought to keep hold of the stanchion. But suddenly they were without strength. He felt as weak as a child. Slowly his body crumpled, hit the next rung of the ladder and then went sailing into space, dead before he hit the sea so far below...

Horrified Honor watched the dead man fly by him. The terrorists were fighting back successfully, he told himself.

He had to get to those explosives now. It wouldn't be long before they started to climb down the rig to set them off and, then on to the moored launch which would take them away from the *Margaret Thatcher*, before the whole massive structure crashed into the sea.

Now, not attempting to drown any noise, bottle in his hand as his only weapon, Major Honor crept through the rig lower and lower. He had some experience of explosives used on the rigs in the old days when he worked in the field and he thought, with luck, he might be able to defuse the lot. Panting a little with the effort, he clambered lower and lower through the white gloom. He could hear the roar of the sea more clearly now and once he thought he saw, in a gap in the fog, the launch moored far below. Then he was there.

He bent hastily and, putting his bottle down beside him, he stared at the pile of explosive heaped around the leg of the rig. 'God Almighty,' he cursed, 'there's a bloody lot of it!' He drew a deep breath and said to himself, 'All right, now let's get on with it.' With fingers that felt like clumsy sausages, he started to work at the first of the fuses, knowing that if he made one mistake, he'd go up – and the rig as well.

'Dusty,' Seal called softly, head turned to one side to catch the slightest sound. Nothing. Just the muted roar of the waves below. Seal bit his bottom lip. First it had been Sergeant Hargreaves, who he always thought was indestructible. Now poor old Dusty, he of the proud boast, 'When I've had a woman, mate, she stays mine. Nobody

can compete with the kind of dong I've got.'
Now apparently that celebrated 'dong'
would never 'pleasure' a woman again.

Seal's face hardened. Now it was up to
him to take revenge. The Special Boat
Service always took care of its own. The
terrorists couldn't expect any mercy from
him now. He pushed on, eyes searching the
white gloom for the first sight of the enemy.

Five minutes later he saw him. The man
was crouched, his back to him, rolling out
some cable. Seal didn't need to be a mind-
reader. The terrorist was running out more
fuse to the explosives that had probably
been stacked further down the rig. They
were getting ready for the final stage of the
attack. Once this was completed, they'd set
the time charges and be off, leaving the rig
to its fate.

Seal crept closer. The terrorist, kneeling
over the fuse, had a Uzi on the stanchion
next to him, within grasping distance of his
right hand. He swallowed hard. He didn't
want to take the man prisoner after what he
and his friends had done to Alpha Team, but
he didn't like the idea of shooting the man

in the back without giving him a chance to defend himself. He supposed it was all part and parcel of the old public school tradition.

He took a deep breath. Then he snapped, 'Stop what you're doing at once – and turn round!' Even as he said the words, he knew the young terrorist wouldn't obey and he was glad, he wouldn't. It would give the opportunity to shoot him in a 'fair' way.

As Dick slowly began to turn, the Palestinian ten metres away hidden in the fog, heard the command. He stiffened and rose carefully from his own length of detonator fuse.

Dick saw the man standing there with his automatic levelled. For a moment he felt a trace of fear. He would die in the next moment, he knew that, but he had to do. He grabbed for the Uzi. Too late. Seal pressed his trigger. Scarlet flame spat from the muzzle of the automatic.

Dick shrieked high and hysterical like a woman. A line of holes like bloody buttons had been stitched across his skinny chest. He staggered. Still he remained upright.

Seal fired again, just one short burst. He didn't want too strong a recoil to make the weapon fire high. Dick flew back, hands to a face that had been shattered to a bloody gore. An instant later, he was tumbling head over heels down the centre of the great rig, heading for the water far below.

The Palestinian cursed. He was alone now. For a while he was wild with rage that Dick had been killed so brutally by the intruder who now stood there, peering into the gloom. Then he pulled himself together and became once again the trained ruthless killer that he had always been.

He calculated his chances coolly and clinically. The crew were still locked up. He had heard nothing of them since the previous day. In essence he was opposed by the single bastard who had killed Dick. But first, before he killed the English bastard, he must ensure that the charges were timed and ready to explode within ten minutes of his reaching the launch.

Then it would be off to the little German coaster that would take him to a remote spot on the Baltic, where his new identity would be waiting for him. Then it would be away from these grim cold northern climes back to his own homeland. This, however, would be the last time.

He could retire on the money they had promised him – the comrade from the *Rote Armee Fraktion* had already passed over a great deal for this particular mission. For a moment he indulged himself. He would fly to Algeria or Morocco, perhaps even Tangiers, where he would find a beautiful willing boy. They were lax about such things there. He would buy the boy pretty things and he would spoil him and they–

The fantasy died a sudden death. There was movement from not far away. It had to be the pig who had killed Dick. He had to get back to the charges without wasting any more time. Moments later he was hurrying down the ladder to where the explosives were.

Major Honor heard him coming. Despite the cold he was lathered in a sweat, as he worked all out on the fuses, his fingers bleeding where the wires had cruelly torn at the flesh. 'Christ,' he gasped to himself as he heard the sounds. What should he do? There was no time to finish the whole job. He had to stop the terrorist getting to the charges.

He stopped work. Shielding his little gold lighter the best he could against the wind, he clicked the wheel. Sparks but no flame. 'Come on,' he cursed, 'come on you bugger – *light!*'

He tried again. Still only sparks. The footsteps were coming ever closer now. Suddenly there was a spurt of red flame. Hastily Major Honor applied it to the ragged bit of cloth. The material spluttered. He puffed on the material, praying he wouldn't be spotted before it was ready. The area of redness grew. It was working.

Up ahead, the Palestinian spotted the sudden spurt of flame. 'Hey,' he broke the silence, 'what are you doing?'

Seal reacted at once. He fired in the direction the sound had come from. Bullets whined and howled off the steel girders. The Palestinian reacted immediately. He fired low from the hip, balancing the Uzi against the right hip bone.

Seal screamed, as the burst of slugs

slammed into his chest and exploded. The light failed completely. He tried to keep upright, but failed miserably. The deck came up, swaying in front of his gaze. He tried to avoid it. He couldn't. It smacked him in the face. His mouth filled with blood. He coughed and spat it out automatically, as he had been trained. He didn't want to choke in his own blood. A red mist threatened to overcome him. There was a loud roaring in his ears. He knew he was going. He craned his neck and peered feebly into the white gloom.

He saw the man who had shot him, Uzi held threateningly in his hand. Some feet behind him was an elderly man, holding a bottle. For some strange reason that he couldn't understand, a little red flame was flickering at the bottle's neck. Then his head slumped forward and he was out.

Chapter Three

Red Ross was angry, very angry. His face was deep red and his eyes sparked furiously. 'I've had a fucking enough,' he announced, slamming another mug of tea on to the steel mess table. 'I'm awash with frigging tea and over the last frigging twenty-four hours I must have eaten half a frigging pig. It's enough to try the patience of a saint, as my old mum used to say.'

There was a murmur of agreement from the others in the smoke-filled mess hall. By now they had forgotten the initial surprise and fear at being hijacked. They'd long finished re-reading all the dog-eared porno mags. Most of them were out of duty-free cigarettes and Red Ross had not allowed them to drink more than a couple of shots of hard liquor over the day.

'The Major's missing. So are those SBS blokes who came in from the Harrier. But there's something going on, 'cos I've just heard the sound of firing.'

'Me, too,' several of the rig's crew agreed.

'So what are we gonna do?' Red Ross asked. He answered his own question. 'We're gonna get out of here. We've still got this day left to bring in the oil. Terrorists or no terrorists, we're gonna do just that. After all, yer all want that fat bonus for Sunday night – tomorrow. Think o' all them fat Hull whoors and all the suds.' He paused and looked around at their faces, as if he were seeing them for the first time and trying to imprint their features on his mind's eye. 'Are yer with me, lads?'

'Ay, ay,' they yelled in unison.

'Then what are we frigging well waiting for? Let's get back to the platform and get the frigging drill started, mates.'

Moments later they were streaming out into the thinning fog, through which the weak, watery wintery sun was trying to break through. Above them the SBS man on guard, shouted, 'Watch it, lads. We've got killers on board, yer know.'

'What d'yer think we are,' Red Ross yelled

back, brandishing a fist like a small steam shovel.

He forgot the SBS guard and yelled above the sudden roar of sea, as the fog started to clear and allow its growl and hiss to ascend up to the platform, 'Come on, get yer backs into it. Yer'll be wanting frigging eggs on yer beer next.'

The men laughed and within five minutes work had commenced once more and down below the drill started to burrow into the rock of the sea bottom, the samples coming up to the platform growing darker and darker by the instant. They weren't far from the gusher now. Red Ross worked them all out, knowing this day would make or break UK Oil. He knew, too, though he wasn't a particularly patriotic man, that it was the same for the old country, too. Oil was Britain's future, its path into the 21st century.

If the *Margaret Thatcher* struck oil today, then more rigs would follow. The oil would flow and with it Britain's wealth would increase. 'Come on, me lucky lads,' he yelled joyfully at the thought, 'get stuck in.

We're frigging well getting there at last!'...

At that very moment the Palestinian was preparing to finish off the wounded Seal. Then he would set the charges and be off down to the launch. Within half an hour it would be all over; and he would be celebrated throughout the Middle East as the man who had avenged the humiliating defeat of Saddam Hussein in *Operation Desert Storm. Operation Stormwind* had brought the battle to the archenemy, England.

He raised his Uzi, taking careful aim as the wounded SBS man lay there helplessly, chest heaving frantically as if he were hyperventilating, but with no sound coming from his gaping mouth, out of the side of which the blood trickled. He took first pressure, his knuckle white, a look of cruel pleasure on his dark, hook nosed face. This would be the last time, he told himself, that he would ever kill anyone and he was going to enjoy that savage primeval sensation: the joy of killing.

The noise behind penetrated his grim pleasurable concentration. He swung round. Too late. The bottle whizzed through the air. It smashed at his feet. *Whoosh!* The Molotov cocktail exploded in a great searing, all consuming flame. It seared his flesh like a gigantic blowtorch. He screamed shrilly. Automatically in his last dying moment, he pressed the trigger of the Uzi. The bullets caught Major Honor completely by surprise. He reeled back, and only at the last minute did he manage to catch on to a stanchion and prevent himself from falling to the North Sea below. He went down on his knees, his breath coming in harsh brittle gasps.

Ten yards away, the Palestinian, panic-stricken and screaming with fear, beat his already burning hands against the burning cloth. Blinded by the mounting flames, he blundered forward, groping his way with an arm that was already blackened and burning, the white bone gleaming like ivory where the flesh had split.

He stumbled and fell to his knees. He was choking. The flames were up about his chest now, burning his face. Suddenly he was blind. Where his eyes had been were now two scarlet suppurating pits. He went down on his face. His struggles became weaker and weaker. For a couple of more times his blackened charred body twitched convulsively. Then he lay still, his shrunken charred head, with the exposed teeth gleaming a tremendous brilliant white, lying in a flickering weak blue flame.

Major Honor was dying, he knew that. But he remained quite rational. Perhaps, he told himself, if he could get to the platform so far above, someone might give him medical help and he would be saved. But he knew it was impossible for him to reach the platform; it would be like trying to reach the moon.

'I could have died in Korea,' he whispered throatily to himself, 'so I've had a good run. Forty years more, old chap.' He sighed and thought of what they had been like then – the survivors. The press had called them the 'Glorious Glosters'. *Bullshit!* he croaked aloud. They hadn't been glorious one bit. They had been proud of themselves, many eighteen-year-old boys, who had grown into men overnight; who had known they had done their duty and had not given in. In his mind's eye, he could still see them, uniform burnt and ragged, faces worn and pared to the bone, but with eyes full of a sense of achievement. How different those boys had been to the ones he knew now, pudgy-faced, wearing baseball caps the wrong way round, dressed in garishly coloured track suits.

Suddenly he felt an overwhelming sadness, as he lay dying there. Perhaps he should have died then on those rocky peaks, with the wrecked equipment scattered everywhere, the khaki-carpet of dead Chinese soldiers littering the slope, the smoke wafting silently over the scene of the last battle, the only sound the soft rumble of the permanent barrage in the distance.

Should he have been left with the dead? Then he wouldn't have had to endure the sight of the country going ever further downhill.

He would have died, feeling that he belonged to something of importance. He sighed and felt the strength ebbing out of him, as if someone had opened a tap. His head lolled to one side. Death was not far away now.

Opposite, the fire that had consumed the Palestinian's body was almost out now. The Palestinian's body had been reduced to the size of a pygmy, a shapeless lump of charred meat. But the little tongues of greedy blue flame were still reaching out in their dying throes. They grew closer and closer to the rest of the charges which major Honor had been unable to defuse, creeping towards them like live things, inch by inch.

Major Honor did not even see them. His eyes were screwed up tight, his face contorted, not with pain but with concentration, as he tried to hear those old tunes of glory for one last time, as they echoed down the years. But they were receding. Fast... Becoming fainter by the instant, almost lost now, gone forever...

The spark touched the explosive. Below, half-way up spud two, there was a dull menacing rumbling. It was low and threatening like the prelude to a thunderstorm. It grew in intensity. Above on the platform the empty coke cans started to roll back and forth. A stanchion crumbled and came tumbling down. A wireless mast cracked, the wires trailing down suddenly and showering the metal deck with angry blue sparks as they touched it. A steel hawser cracked and hissed through the air like an angry silver whip.

Red Ross caught the abrupt panic he saw on the faces of the deck crew in time. 'Stand by ... stand by, the lot of yer!' he yelled at the top of his voice, as the low rumbling grew in strength by the instant, rising to a banshee-like howling and keening, that set the small hairs at the backs of their heads standing erect.

'We're going under!' someone screamed in panic. 'Oh my God, we're going–'

His panic-stricken cry ended abruptly as Red Ross punched him in the jaw. 'Shut yer bloody trap!' he cried furiously. 'All of yer shut yer jaws. We're not fucking going under.'

The rig lurched suddenly and frighteningly. Piping came tumbling down and great drums of diesel clattered across the suddenly tilted platform, so that the men had to jump hastily to one side as they rolled past and over the edge, falling into the sea far below.

Automatically Red followed their progress as they tumbled to the water, but as he did so, he saw something else. The sea was heaving and bubbling in a white fury, as the platform under his feet tilted to an alarming thirty degree angle. By sheer will-power Red Ross kept himself on his feet, while all about him men were thrown off their feet or clutched wildly for support to prevent the same happening to them. Was it, he asked himself, hardly daring to ask that over-whelming question. 'Fellers,' he began with a roar, 'I think–'

He never ended the sentence. He broke off abruptly, his mouth gaping open foolishly with astonishment like that of some village idiot. A thin yellow-black rain, which the happy men later described looking like, 'ferking shit when yer've got the trots', was falling out of the sky and turning their outfits that same obscene colour. Red Ross stared up at the yellow-black drizzle, letting it fall on his upturned face, not daring to believe the evidence of his own eyes.

He looked over the side of the rig once

more to confirm what he thought was happening. Two hundred yards away just on the other side of the remaining fog bank, the sea had gone absolutely crazy. Huge bubbles of trapped gas were exploding noisily on the surface. Geysers sprang fifty feet in the air. Spume lashed the damaged legs of the rig. *All were black – blacker than black.*

Red Ross's eyes filled with wonder – and tears. He didn't know whether to laugh or cry. It had all taken so long, so much heartbreak, so many lives. But it was there all right. Yes, it was there.

Finally, after what seemed an age, he found his voice. To him, even as he spoke it seemed strangely disjointed like that of someone else. 'Jesus wept,' he cried, clenching his big fists, 'the old *Margaret Thatcher's* done it at frigging last!'

They stared at him, as if they could not comprehend his words.

His voice rose, crying against the howl of the wind and that great black stream which was getting thicker by the moment. 'Don't you understand, you soft pricks?' he cried, as the thick rain drenched him, slushing down his massive body in viscous fury. *'Oil ... we've struck oil at last ....!'*

AFTERMATH

'Gatsby believed in the green light, the orgiastic future that year by year recedes before us. It eluded us then, but that's no matter – tomorrow we can run faster, stretch our arms further ... and one fine morning– So we bear on, boats against the current, borne ceaselessly into the past'.

F. Scott Fitzgerald: The Great Gatsby, *1926*

'You wait till we get down there,' Yates, the
other surviving member of Alpha Team, was
saying with drunken energy. 'In all that heat.
Hell, they'll be ripping off their jumpers and
flashing their tits before yer can say Jack
Robinson. Better than Benidorm any day
with all them German grannies with their
tired tits.' He took another gulp of the
unaccustomed champagne and handed the
empty glass to the waiter with, 'fill her up
mate.'

The waiter looked disdainfully down his
long nose, while Yates waited cheerfully,
eyeing one of the 'honoured guests' who
had bent down too low in too short a skirt
and was showing much more of her
anatomy than was really wise. The SBS man
took the glass, said, 'ta' to the waiter from
The Savoy and whispered, 'lovely bit of
grub that. Legs right up to her arse.'

'I wouldn't know, sir,' the waiter said
haughtily and made his escape as swiftly as

his dignity allowed him to.

Seal, his right arm still in a sling after two months, said, 'Yates, old chap, do keep it down to a dull roar. After all this *is* The Savoy, you know.'

'Ay, where all the big nobs hang out like in the heads. Get it, sir?' He saw the look in Captain Seal's eyes and decided it would be wiser to keep it down to a 'dull roar', after all.

All around them there was the clink of glasses, the brittle patter of an upper class cocktail party, the occasional bursts of hearty VIP laughter, rich and unrestrained, full of its own importance.

Seal frowned. In the old days when he had been younger he had enjoyed 'bashes', as they had called them then, of this kind. Now he no longer did. They reminded him that people of this type had lost contact with the real world or didn't care, as long as they could go leading their own careless, complicated lives till the money and good times ran out.

He spotted Hilary on the arm of Red Ross, who looked decidedly out of place in this company, awkward in a suit, collar and tie. He waved. They spotted him and started to work their way through the throng towards him, and Yates, who was gazing in awe down the cleavage of an expensively gowned woman, who dripped with diamonds. 'Hell's bells,' he moaned to himself, licking his lips as if in anticipation of a good meal, 'all that meat and no potatoes.'

Hilary looked thinner and her pallor was emphasized by the black she still wore, in respect to the dead Major Honor. She had visited Seal three times at Hasler while he had been recovering from his wounds and on the very last visit she had broken down and sobbed, 'Oh, I did so love him! How sad he couldn't have seen how things worked out for UK oil.'

Now she was constrained and fully in charge of herself. She planted a light kiss on his cheek and he caught a whiff of her perfume and liked it. Red Ross followed by reaching out his massive paw to shake his hand, saying, 'I'd like to say thank you for what you and yer blokes did, Captain.'

Seal looked at the hand and said, 'Nice

and gentle, old friend, I'm barely recovered you know.'

Red Ross laughed and did as he was commanded.

Red Ross stopped the waiter and said gruffly, 'A beer please. Newcastle Brown Ale if yer've got it.'

'We don't serve beer at the Sav–' the waiter began, then he saw the look in the big Yorkshireman's eyes and added, 'I'll see what I can do sir.'

'You do that,' Red said easily. 'But don't make it too long, eh?'

The waiter sniffed.

Seal took Hilary to one side and left Yates and Red Ross to chat together for a while. 'How's it going?' he asked, his gaze still taking in the moneyed crowd of oilmen from all over the world and their backers. It was his turn to sniff at the sight.

'All right. The company's well on its feet again. The capital's there and Red Ross is going to run our newest venture.'

'Newest?'

'Yes, the *Major Honor*,' she announced with a note of pride in her voice. 'The biggest rig ever built. At least there will be something to remember him by.' Suddenly there was the sheen of tears in her eyes.

Instinctively he pressed her hand and felt somehow that his warmth was being returned.

De Boers rapped a spoon on a champagne flute for attention. Slowly the brittle chatter died away, and all eyes turned in his direction. The Dutchman smiled at them and said, using his standard opening, 'Ladies and gentlemen, I am of the three Ss school of public speaking.' He paused for the expected look of bewilderment, before explaining, 'That is *stand* up, *shout* up and *shut* up.'

There was some polite laughter and Yates grumbled drunkenly, 'Ay, well I hope he keeps to the last part.' He took another drink.

'I thought,' De Boers continued, 'I would report to you, my friends, – *briefly* – on UK Oil's current situation. As they say in the oil business, God put the stuff – oil – in the earth 150 million years, so you can't expect to get it out in a couple of days. But,' he

343

smiled gently at them, 'we have succeeded doing exactly that with the *Margaret Thatcher*. Now we've just put the *Major Honor* into commission–'

Hilary winced slightly at the mention of the beloved name, and Seal pressed her hand harder.

'And I'm totally confident that it won't take her 150 million years to come on stream, however we shall continue to run at a loss. But I will say this,' De Boers' voice rose powerfully, 'by this time next year, UK Oil will be providing a dividend to its shareholders.' He beamed at his listeners.

There was polite applause and he waited till it was over, which was not very long, then he said, raising his own glass of champagne, 'I'd like you to charge your glasses.' As if by magic the waiters appeared from nowhere, silver trays heavy with glasses of champagne.

De Boers waited till they all had glasses and then said, 'Ladies and gentlemen, I give you the future. Financial success to UK Oil.' He grinned and added, 'Here's to money!'

'*Here's to money!*' his listeners, all members or shareholders of UK Oil, cried back enthusiastically.

Then people laughed and giggled, as if it were all great fun.

'*Here's to money!*' the Brig, who with Daisy, had just joined the little group with Seal, echoed the words scornfully. 'As if *that's* what it is all about, eh.'

Seal glanced at the Brigadier. He looked younger and happier, and Daisy didn't look as sick as she had used to look. She wasn't chainsmoking either. He wondered idly if the two of them were living together. He hoped they were. They both needed someone to cling to, he told himself.

The Brig forced a wintry smile. 'Well, let them have their money.' He looked urgently around their keen faces, knowing that they felt the way he did. 'We have other things in mind. We've all had our R and R,* and now there's something new on the cards.' The Brig's eyes gleamed.

They leaned forward to hear better and then

* Rest and Recuperation leave

345

Daisy said, 'The game's afoot, eh, just like old Watson used to say to Sherlock?'

'Exactly,' the Brig snapped and lowered his voice even more. 'It's the damned Frogs...'

All around the chatter continued. Everyone seemed to be drinking, faces becoming more and more flushed, and repeating the same word over and over again, repeating it with a kind of almost sexual desire animating their feature. *'Money ... money ... money...'*

Ten minutes later the Brigadier's group left. No one seemed to notice them go. Perhaps no one was interested. It was still *money ... money ... money...*

They left the forecourt to The Savoy and passed into the thin wintry sunshine. Opposite a paperseller, banner headline wrapped around his waist, was crying the words written on it, *'New War in the Balkans French threaten to pull out... New War in the Balkans...'*

'Time's running out,' the Brigadier said, almost as if speaking to himself and then they vanished, a handful of anonymous people, into the London crowds...

The publishers hope that this book has given you enjoyable reading. Large Print Books are especially designed to be as easy to see and hold as possible. If you wish a complete list of our books please ask at your local library or write directly to:

Magna Large Print Books
Magna House, Long Preston,
Skipton, North Yorkshire.
BD23 4ND

This Large Print Book for the partially sighted, who cannot read normal print, is published under the auspices of

THE ULVERSCROFT FOUNDATION

Other MAGNA Titles In Large Print

Other MAGNA Titles
In Large Print

LYN ANDREWS
Angels Of Mercy

HELEN CANNAM
Spy For Cromwell

EMMA DARCY
The Velvet Tiger

SUE DYSON
Fallfield Rose

J.M. GREGSON
To Kill A Wife

MEG HUTCHINSON
A Promise Given

JEM WILSON
A Singing Grove

RICHARD WOODMAN
The Cruise Of The Commissioner